THE

'You'd
began to
again. A
start up
ground,
away to ... , level space a short distance from the site office. The bucket began to lower until it rested on the ground. As far as I could see, it was full of soil. I looked up at Stanley and as I did so the bucket began to tilt. The soil started to slither out in a dusty trickle that became a rush, and we were all covered in the cloud of dust that arose – me, Tommy, and the dozen or so men who had gathered round to see what it was that had affected Stanley so much. When the dust had cleared, all I could see was a pile of soil, and I reached for the shovel one of the men had in his hands. I poked at the pile, and as I did so a large lump of earth tumbled slowly away from the rest of the soil. Beneath it was what had disturbed Stanley. I wasn't surprised. It was enough to disturb anyone. After all it isn't every day you dig up a skeleton.

THE ROSE MEDALLION

James Grant

THE ROSE MEDALLION

ISBN 0 600 37619 2

First published in Great Britain 1977
by Frederick Muller Limited
Hamlyn Paperbacks edition 1979

Hamlyn Paperbacks are published by
The Hamlyn Publishing Group Ltd,
Astronaut House,
Feltham,
Middlesex, England

Set, printed and bound in Great Britain by
Cox & Wyman Ltd,
London, Reading and Fakenham

CHAPTER ONE

'Harry. Wake up, Harry it's late.'

I screwed up my eyes and prayed that he would go away. He didn't. A hand, the size of a fox terrier, gripped my shoulder and shook me. My teeth rattled and the part of my brain immediately behind my eyes, the part the booze always gets to first, seemed to detach itself from the rest of the cerebrum. I opened my eyes and shouted. Not words, it was too early in the day for that, just noises. Stanley stood there, towering over the bed, half-crouched but still towering, smiling with unconcealed delight that I had survived to live another day. I swung my legs over the edge of the bed and felt around for my trousers. Stanley handed them to me, then my shirt. I wondered what had happened to my underpants and then realised I still wore them. I thought about changing them and decided against it. I didn't plan on having an accident that day. I pulled on the trousers and, carrying the shirt, I walked through into the bathroom, cleaned my teeth and made a gesture at washing. I decided to postpone shaving until I reached the office. On the way back to my bedroom I looked into Stanley's to see if he had made his bed. He had. The blankets were folded in a neat pile and rested on the floor beside the mattresses. He didn't have a real bed. If I had been rich I would have had a bed made for him, but I wasn't rich, and as standard beds were too small and too weak he made do with a small mountain of mattresses on the floor. He didn't seem to mind. He was still in my bedroom smiling gently.

'Is the kettle on?' I asked him. He shook his head, the smile dimming for an instant. 'Then put it on for Christ's sake,' I yelled. The smile returned in full brilliance to show that he knew I wasn't really cross with him and he went out of the room, still half-crouched in the way he usually walked in the house. It saved him the trouble of having to duck his head every time he went through a door. I finished dressing and followed him through to the kitchen. The kettle was on and I lifted the lid to make sure he had remembered to fill it. He had, which made a change. I found two relatively unstained mugs and dropped tea-bags into them and thought about breakfast. I decided that food was the last thing I wanted, but that still left Stanley. I opened the fridge door and looked inside. It wasn't very inspiring. 'Omelette?' I asked.

'Sure, Harry, anything.'

I nodded and reached into the cupboard above the fridge for a basin. I broke six eggs into it and handed it to Stanley together with a fork. He began to stir them with that gentleness which he could bring to anything when he chose, a gentleness that was completely out of proportion to his enormous size and was a never-ending source of surprise to me. The frying pan already had a thick coating of congealed fat in it and I put it on to the cooker top and lit the gas under it. The kettle boiled and I poured water into the two mugs and stirred the tea-bags around, watching Stanley as I did so. The basin of eggs had his full attention as did anything he was given to do. The smile was still there but complicated by the slight frown of concentration.

Stanley is my cousin. I look after him. Well, someone has to and there isn't anyone else. His mother and mine were sisters. They were very close; they met and married two cousins; they even had a double wedding. Stanley was born three weeks after me. I'm told my birth was easy. Stanley's wasn't – his mother died. After that he came to live with us. There was never any suggestion that he should be fostered or adopted; those were foreign words. My mother simply added him to the Morgan household and his father contributed what he could towards the family budget. It wasn't very much as Jack Meadows was out of work more often than he was in. Then one day he got a job, on a ship, and that was the last we saw of him. Stanley was five and I think the family, that is to say the adults in the family, had already begun to suspect the truth about him. I hadn't of course, to me Stanley was simply the boy I was growing up with, even though he was growing at a much more rapid rate than me.

I'm not certain when it was that I first realised that Stanley was different. Probably it was when I was about ten or eleven, when we had to change schools because my father had moved to Leicester from Lincoln. The boys at the local school had known Stanley and me from the beginning and there had never been any trouble. At the new school the sudden arrival in mid-term of two new boys had brought us more attention than might otherwise have been the case. Most of that attention had been directed towards Stanley. By then he already towered over me and all the other ten- and eleven-year olds. At first there had been a degree of respect in the attitude of the other boys, and then they had begun to see that the ever-present smile and the total inability to comprehend even the simplest of lessons concealed something I hadn't known. Or if I had, I had chosen to ignore it. Stanley was simple-minded. That was the way it was phrased in those days. The other boys had begun to probe and soon discovered that Stanley's gentle smile concealed nothing that could cause them any problems. Beneath it he was as gentle and unassuming as he appeared to be from the surface. That finished us of course. You know what boys of that age are like. They had begun to torment Stanley. Cautiously at first and then, as he had failed to protect himself, with increasing bravado and savagery. There are few things quite as savage as a ten-year-old boy, or girl, for that matter, because they joined in too. And, of course, being human, I had gradually sided with the mob. It must have been a very bad time for Stanley but he had remained unconcerned, still smiling, still gentle, and still devoted to me. I must have been a heartless little bastard.

'Harry.'

I looked round with a start. Stanley was holding up the basin of beaten eggs. I took it from him and poured the eggs into the frying pan. I fished out the tea-bags from the mugs and added milk and sugar and handed one to Stanley. He sat in his special, reinforced chair, the mug like a toy in his hands, smiling at nothing in particular. I looked at his hands, and remembered the day he had first used the strength that was in them.

We had been at school for nearly two years and most of that time had been unremitting torture for Stanley. The change had come one day when for some reason, so trivial I can no longer remember what it was, the pack had turned on me. There had been about eight of them and they had been giving me a good working-over. Then Stanley had appeared and had asked them in his quiet way to let me go. This had given them a new target and they had turned on him but he hadn't seemed to mind in the least. One of the pack, Tommy Andrews, suddenly sensing that they were doing what Stanley wanted, had ordered four of the gang to hold Stanley while the others had turned their attention to me. Two had held me and the remaining two, Tommy and another boy, who would have been big in any circle that hadn't included Stanley, had begun to punch me in that painful, non-damaging way of children. Abruptly there had been a bellowing roar, and twisting my head I had seen the remarkable sight of four small boys flying into the air simultaneously, and Stanley emerging from beneath the flailing arms and legs. His smile had still been there, but only on his lips. The four who had been attacking me had put up a small show of resistance but Stanley had flicked them to one side, almost casually, even the big one. Suddenly there were no longer eight against two. There were just three of us there – Stanley, myself and Tommy Andrews. Stanley had seized hold of Tommy; his hands, already big, had wrapped around his throat and I believe, even now over thirty years later, that he would have killed Tommy, but something in me reacted and, instead of letting Stanley wreak the vengeance I had felt I deserved, I had yelled at him to stop. He did. Not at first, and not before Tommy's face had turned a dark red, and the alarm in his eyes had been replaced by real fear. After that Stanley was never taunted again and I was treated with considerably more respect than I deserved. And, of course, I became Stanley's keeper. Not that I was aware of it then but looking back, as I often did, that was when it began. Just as he had protected me I had sensed that I had to protect him, not in the same way of course, but he needed me.

I shovelled Stanley's breakfast on to a plate and sat watching him eat it. It would be wrong to say he ate like a horse; he ate steadily throughout his waking hours, seldom a massive meal but also seldom letting more than an hour pass between snacks. And one of Stanley's snacks would have kept me going for a day.

Oddly enough the episode in the school playground had had a salutary effect upon Tommy Andrews, and he cautiously became a friend of mine and of Stanley's. A useful friend too as it turned out. Years later, as Stanley and I had drifted around the country, we had met Tommy again and he had given us jobs. Then when I had grown bored he had told me with unconcealed glee that he was pleased, because he didn't really want me but he did need Stanley. After some thought

I had come to the conclusion that unwittingly I had stumbled into a situation that gave me what I needed – a regular job for Stanley which allowed me to get on with my own life, at least during working hours. There were only two snags. One was that Tommy's job kept him moving about the country; he was a civil engineer, a site agent. The other snag was that I hadn't known how I wanted to spend my life. As a result I drifted from job to job scraping a living, and for a long time suffering the indignity of relying upon Stanley's earnings. They were substantial too. Tommy had discovered that Stanley had a gift with things mechanical. Ostensibly he was a driver on the sites Tommy ran. He drove anything, cars, vans, lorries, tractors, Drotts, 'dozers, JCBs, anything at all, and when something broke down Stanley could coax it back into service, those huge hands performing minor mechanical miracles that saved money and, most important for Tommy, time. Eventually I took a part-time job that gave me a direction. The job was as a debt-collector for a small agency, and after I had been with them for a few months I was approached by a larger firm who offered me more money to do the same thing for them. It was the first time anyone, apart from Tommy, had offered me a job and I had taken it, and very soon I was offered even more money to extend my work into other fields. The firm had other departments and one of them was an inquiry agency, and I seemed to fit into their operation as if I had been doing it all my life. I suppose it was a combination of an inquiring mind, a great deal of patience with people – I'd learned that living with Stanley – and a natural ability to sense when people were telling me the truth and when they were not. When Tommy moved on and Stanley and I followed, I decided to stay in that line of business, and at Tommy's suggestion and with the help of his bank account I set up on my own. Moving from town to town didn't help a lot, but fortunately Tommy's jobs were usually big ones and we stayed in places for a year or two at a time. This had been our longest stay; Tommy had been working on the site of the new hospital in Guildford, and after that he had gone on to the M25 extension running west from Cobham. This had meant that I had been able to build up quite a steady little business from my office in Guildford.

In case you wonder what the respectable residents of Guildford wanted with a private inquiry agent, then rest assured that just as many children and wives and husbands left home there as anywhere else. More, probably. The deserted spouses and the distracted parents came to me in the twin beliefs: one mistaken, that I could do more than the police could do; the other correct, that the police were too busy trying to stem the crime rate to chase after people who chose, usually quite rationally, to leave home. That was my forte, tracing people, people who didn't want to be traced but who others wanted traced for their own good – for the good of the inquirers that is, seldom for the good of the missing person. I was realistic enough to believe that if someone went missing they did it for good reasons, at least reasons that seemed good enough to them.

I took the empty plate from Stanley and swilled it under the tap. 'More tea?' I asked him. He shook his head and glanced anxiously at the clock.

'We'll be late, Harry,' he told me. I nodded and for the hundredth time that year I didn't bother to tell him that it didn't matter. It did, to him.

'Get the van out,' I told him and he bounded up and out of the door with a lightness and agility that never failed to amaze me. I heard him open the garage doors and moments later the Transit started up and purred softly out into the driveway. The Ford Motor Company would have been proud of that van. With Stanley's deft touch it ran as sweetly and as silently as an electric clock, and on an open road when there were no police cars to spoil the fun it could make even an XJS owner think it was time for an overhaul.

I picked up my case and walked out into the fresh air. It *was* fresh too. Shackleford village stands less than half a mile from the A3, but that was far enough to make it free from the smell and the sound of traffic. It was pretty too; most of the houses were built of stone, and most of the owners vied with one another for the best displays of flowers that grew inside, outside and on top of garden walls. It was expensive to live there, if you were an owner that is. We rented; that wasn't particularly cheap either but we had special terms. One of the first jobs I had done when I had come to Guildford had restored to the family bosom a slightly spotty youth who dreamed of better things than the family could offer him. Just what was better than a detached house in twenty acres of woodland and pasture with half a dozen horses, a four-car garage and a swimming pool, I never did discover. The pool even had a roof for bad-weather bathing. Still, it takes all sorts. Some people don't know when they're well off. Anyway the family's gratitude extended beyond my fee, and they offered me one of the cottages they owned at a reduced rent for as long as I wanted it. They had already learned of my enforced fidgety feet so they were not being too generous.

I climbed into the van beside Stanley and we slid smoothly out into the lane and turned towards the Hog's Back. On the way we passed the Cyder House where I had spent more of the previous evening than was good for me. I made a mental note to call in and see if I had left with more on the slate than I should have done. When we came up on to the Hog's Back the traffic was thickening, ready for the onslaught on the A3, but I concentrated instead on the view. One of the great failings of Surrey is that although it is one of the most beautiful of English counties there are very few places where you can see more than a little bit of it at a time. The main Farnham to Guildford road across the top of the Hog's Back was one of the few places. In too few minutes we were embroiled in the stream of uni-directional metallic pirhana fish snapping and jostling their way towards London. I closed my eyes and pretended they were not there. I dozed for about three-quarters of an hour, until I felt the van make a left turn that told me we were nearing the site where Stanley, when he wasn't saving Tommy a fortune in maintenance costs, would shift muck, as civil engineers so charmingly phrase it. We lurched through the site gateway, the van wheels spinning in the dry dusty furrows ploughed during the winter and wet spring. The contractors were slowly slashing through the pleasant wooded countryside with a long, narrow, treeless scar of reddish-brown earth which was gradually being covered by its protecting strip of grey six-lane concrete.

Stanley climbed out of the van and stood beaming at me as I slid over into his seat. I wrestled with the mechanism that allowed me to pull the seat far enough forward so that I could reach the pedals. When I looked up, Tommy had appeared, and was grinning at me from beside Stanley. Tommy's head came up to Stanley's shoulder, and Tommy wasn't small. In fact he was several inches taller than me, and I'm no midget.

'Lowering yourself still I see,' he called. I didn't feel like talking so I showed him two fingers and reversed out of the site gates, narrowly avoiding knocking down the sign that said 'No reversing out of site gates' signed 'T. Andrews, Site Agent'. I glanced back at Tommy and saw that my little manoeuvre had, as I had hoped, removed the smile from his face.

I drove back towards Guildford. Most of the traffic was still fighting its way to London and there was comparatively little going my way. I turned off the main road and went down the old road into Ripley, and stopped at the garage where what remained of my Victor estate car was piled into a corner of the forecourt. They told me the insurance company's man had been the previous afternoon, and had officially written off the car as a total loss. That hadn't surprised me. They tried half-heartedly to sell me another car, but I wasn't in a car buying mood, and I climbed into the van and drove back up to the main road and on into Guildford.

My car had been stolen three nights earlier, and the joy-riding thief and his companions, two young girls, had gone to the big Borstal in the sky after a head-on crash with a container lorry. When I saw the wreckage, they had already removed the bits of thief and friends, but the remains of the seats had changed from light-green to brown, and I had needed all my will-power to avoid throwing up all over the debris.

I turned the van into one of the side streets off Woodbridge Road, and tried to decide whether I would be in the office long enough to warrant putting it into the car park. As far as I was aware there was nothing waiting for me, and I would very probably spend most of the day touting around solicitors' offices in the faint hope that they might have some business for me. That would be best done on foot for the joint reasons that, like everywhere else, Guildford has a parking problem, and a private detective in a Ford Transit van doesn't do a lot to inspire confidence – no disrespect to the van. I carried on until I reached the Quarry car park and drove down into it. A multi-storey car park you drive *down* into shows that planners can sometimes get it right. In Guildford's case it almost made up for the new main Post Office – almost, but not quite.

On the way to the office I walked into the insurance company and talked to them about the car. They seemed to think that twelve hundred was about right and I couldn't really argue. It seemed fair, and if I could find something that was more or less roadworthy for less than a thousand,

Stanley would be able to turn it into a reliable vehicle, and leave me with enough to pay a few bills that were beginning to curl up at the edges.

The office was much as I had left it the night before. A few more grammes of dust had settled on the floor and furniture, and I decided to speak gently to the old lady who supplemented her pension by waving her duster at the dust twice a week. There was also some post: two buff envelopes which I decided to open later when I felt stronger, and a white one that was of a quality you don't see all that often – at least not in my business. I opened it and read the letter. It was a job, nothing spectacular but a job. A lady in Devon had a daughter who had broken an unspecified family tradition and joined the army. Like most girls who join the army she had come to the barracks in Guildford and then, after a while, she had decided she agreed with the family. It *had* been a mistake, and the modern army being what it is she had got out without undue fuss and bother. But she hadn't gone home. Mother seemed to think that was because she was ashamed to admit she had been wrong. From her letter Mother seemed to be a reasonable sort and she was probably right. Anyway it didn't affect me one way or the other. It was a job, and I telephoned the old girl, told her my fees, to which she agreed, and asked her a few questions and told her to send me a photograph of the girl with her retaining cheque. Then I rang the commanding officer at the barracks. She seemed as concerned as the mother had been, and agreed that I could go up there and talk to some of the missing girl's companions. I walked up to the barracks, which wasn't all that far from the office, and talked to the commanding officer and four or five of the girls. I came away with a few leads and a feeling of deep depression. Why a life in the army should seem to be such a waste for a girl when it didn't for a boy escaped me, but it did.

Back at the office I made a few telephone calls, and

eventually turned up a guy in south-east London who seemed to know more than he was prepared to tell me. I told him a lie about the girl's age and he went into shock. When he recovered the power of speech he told me where she was living and I telephoned her mother, who told me she would drive up immediately, and as she hadn't yet posted my cheque she would come via Guildford and deliver it in person. I did a mental calculation, and decided that unless she drove faster than Concorde flew she wouldn't make it before I would have gone for the day. She said she would call anyway and leave the cheque in the letter-box. I said she was very kind and we hung up in a flurry of mutual thanks and gratitude.

It was about four in the afternoon when the telephone rang. When I answered it Tommy Andrews was yelling in my ear before I had time to open my mouth.

'Get down here! For Christ's sake get down here!'

'What's happened?' I asked.

'Your bloody cousin, that's what,' he said ungrammatically and unhelpfully.

'Stanley?' I asked.

'Of course,' he yelped. 'How many other bloody cousins have you got who work for me?' It suddenly occurred to me that it was quite a lot of years since I had heard Tommy get upset, and an image of Stanley as a boy trying to strangle him floated into my mind.

'Okay, Tommy,' I said, 'I'll be there as soon as I can. Hold on a moment though.' I paused until I was sure I had his attention. 'Has anyone been hurt?'

When he answered he was calmer. 'No, of course not.' He must have thought the same thoughts as I did. 'Stanley hasn't done anything to anyone.'

'Then what's happened?'

'I don't bloody know,' he said. 'He's sitting in a muckshifter right in front of the office, and he won't come down out of the cab, and he won't let anyone else up there. All he'll say is that he won't move until you come. For Christ's sake, Harry, the whole site's come to a stop. Everybody is standing around looking at him. Get here fast, will you.'

'Okay,' I told him and replaced the receiver. I locked the office door and walked back to the car park. The moment of panic I had felt when I thought that Stanley might be doing something damaging to someone had passed, but it had left in my mind the uneasiness that I had been made to feel on two other occasions since that day in the school yard when Stanley had almost terminated Tommy's life.

One of them had been just after I had been told by the medical board that I was unfit to serve King and Country as a National Serviceman, due to a respiratory condition I hadn't even known I had. It had been something of a relief because I hadn't particularly wanted to go. Stanley had been failed on the grounds that, although he was fitter and stronger than any two other conscripts put together, he could barely understand the simplest of orders. That, together with his inability to read or write much more than 'The cat sat on the mat' had made the medical board accept that he was below their not very high standards as a target suitable for enemy bullets. It had suddenly come to me that I had lost the chance of escaping for two years from my enforced protectorship of Stanley, and I had gone out and got drunk. We were living in Walsall at the time. My parents had died in Leicester within a few months of one another, and Stanley and I had started the drifting that was to continue until we met Tommy Andrews again. I had been ejected from one pub, and had managed to get into another with less arbitrary rules of exclusion. There had been a crowd of hard-drinking locals in there, talking in their thick nasal accents, and somewhere along the line I had joined in the conversation and they hadn't liked that, and they had liked even less the things I had said. I couldn't remember afterwards what I had said, but it had been enough to upset them. They had followed me outside, and a few yards down the road they had pulled me into the yard of an empty shop and had started to give me a lesson in manners, to say nothing of a lesson in how to hurt a man. Then out of nowhere Stanley had appeared and suddenly bodies were flying everywhere. I don't know how many he took on, at least six, and none of them had seemed incapable of looking after himself. At least they had seemed capable of looking after themselves against normal opposition. Stanley wasn't normal. He didn't do it the way he had in the school playground; he seemed to have more control, until he got to the last one. He picked him up and wrapped his long arms around him and squeezed. I sobered up quickly then and eventually managed to make him drop the man.

I read the report in the newspapers. Later they described it as a gang fight, implying that there had been the same number on each side; the men Stanley had attacked had obviously given false information to the police. Their reputations would have suffered if it had become common knowledge that they had been torn apart by one man. We left town within the week.

It was several years later that we had the second bit of bother, and I still don't like to think about that.

It took me about half an hour to reach the site near Cobham. There was little traffic, and what there was was mostly coming towards me as the nightly rush to get out of London began. When I turned into the site I saw Tommy's problem. Just inside and to the left was the site office: a conglomeration of nissen huts, prefabricated sheds, wheeled caravans, and all the usual random bits and pieces that make up a site office on any construction site in the country. In front of the office was a huge bright yellow machine. Its big bucket was as high in the air as it would go, and sitting impassively in the cab was Stanley. Tommy saw me arrive and stamped over the ground towards me, his feet kicking up little puffs of dust. I climbed out of the Transit and went to meet him. 'Tell me what happened,' I said.

'He was clearing muck down the site.' Tommy gestured with his left arm towards where the scar of earthworks disappeared through the remains of a once-peaceful wood. 'About half past two he brought the machine back here. He stopped there, where he is now, and he won't move. He hasn't said anything except to ask for you. He hasn't looked up, down or bloody sideways.' Tommy looked at me speculatively for a moment. 'I hope he hasn't gone, well, I hope he isn't . . .'

'I expect there's a good reason for it, Tommy,' I told him with more conviction than I felt. Somewhere inside me there had always been the fear that one day Stanley would go out of his mind. Not that there was any reason why he should; his was not that kind of mind. It was, in fact, a perfectly normal mind; it had been slow in developing for the first fifteen years of his life and then it had stopped altogether. I walked over to the bulldozer and looked up. Stanley was staring straight ahead and as far as I could see he wasn't smiling, which didn't do a lot to improve my state of mind. I clambered up on to the tracks of the machine and then up to the cab. I pulled open the door and reached in to touch him on his leg. He looked down at me and after a moment his eyes focused on my face, and his smile slowly returned without completely removing the shadow from his eyes.

'Hello Harry,' he said.

'Hello Stanley,' I said. 'Can I come in?'

He looked at me in surprise. 'Yes. What are you doing here, Harry? Is it time to go home?'

I swung myself up beside him. In the confined space of the cab his massive bulk seemed greater than ever. Dressed as he was, with his sleeves rolled up on to his biceps, and with his heavy check shirt opened down almost to the waist, so that his pectoral muscles bulged out, he looked as if he might very well be the strongest man in the world. His body had expanded to match his frame, and he had a muscular development that would have made him a certain winner in any body-building contest, with little more preparation than a quick rub over with some baby oil.

'No,' I told him. 'It isn't time to go home. Not yet. Not until you've finished with this load.' I gestured towards the bucket that was still high above my head. He looked out of the window and stared at the bucket as if he was seeing it for the first time. Then the smile faltered. He turned and looked at me.

'I didn't do it, Harry,' he said and there was a pathetic urgency in his voice that gripped me.

'Okay, Stanley, I know that. Now what's happened?' He raised one hand and pointed to the bucket.

'In there,' he said. I looked up at the bucket. I could see nothing. From that angle I couldn't even see whether it was full or empty.

'You'd better let me see,' I said, and began to clamber down to the ground again. Above me I heard the engine start up and then, as I reached the ground, the machine moved slowly away to a clear, level space a short distance from the site office. The bucket began to lower until it rested on the ground. As far as I could see, it was full of soil. I looked up at Stanley and as I did so the bucket began to tilt. The soil started to slither out in a dusty trickle that became a rush, and we were all covered in the cloud of dust that arose – me, Tommy, and the dozen or so men who had gathered round to see what it was that had affected Stanley so much. When the dust had cleared, all I could see was a pile of soil, and I reached for the shovel one of the men had in his hands. I poked at the pile, and as I did so a large lump of earth tumbled slowly away from the rest of the soil. Beneath it was what had disturbed Stanley. I wasn't surprised. It was enough to disturb anyone. After all it isn't every day you dig up a skeleton.

CHAPTER TWO

The police came and asked questions and took photographs and measurements, and made lots of notes. Most of their questions were directed at Stanley, but they were simply to help them locate the exact point where he had dug up the skeleton, and where he had tipped the loads of earth he had dug up immediately before that particular one. I stayed with Stanley after I had convinced the police that they wouldn't get very far if I didn't stay. He had shown them the exact spot, and he had been able to tell them precisely where the preceding loads had been dumped. One thing about Stanley was that he was systematic. Then, when they were sure they couldn't learn anything more, they had fenced off the area where Stanley had been working, and the area outside the office where he had tipped the skeleton, and had allowed the site to try and get back to normal.

In any event by the time the police had finished talking to everyone, Tommy had closed the site for that day, the light was beginning to go, and we all went home. I drove the Transit because I wasn't too sure how Stanley was feeling. I had told Tommy that I would probably keep Stanley with me for a couple of days, and he seemed to think it was a good idea. When he had realised that Stanley's odd behaviour had been for a good cause he had resumed his usual amiable cynicism, and he had said nothing more about Stanley's mind. In fact he suggested I keep Stanley off until the following Monday, adding that he wouldn't stop his pay. The following morning I thought at first that Stanley had forgotten all about the discovery of the previous day, which wouldn't have surprised me, but he hadn't. Around eleven, when I had just finished telling him that we would be going down to the bird zoo in the afternoon, he asked me in all innocence if he could keep the skeleton for his collection. I told him he couldn't and he didn't seem disturbed, just disappointed.

Stanley's collection was a thing of never-ending delight to him and a permanent source of irritation to me. Wherever he worked he collected things; not useful, re-saleable things but odds and ends that, with the best will in the world, could not be described as anything other than rubbish. His bedroom was filled with them, and so was the spare room, and the outbuildings, and a caravan we had lived in at one time and still kept for emergencies. There were all sorts of things in the collection: old car tyres, pieces of metal and lumps of wood, discarded pans and pieces of refrigerators, plastic milk-bottle crates and old pram wheels; anything in fact that was of no value to anyone at all. Anyone, that is, except Stanley.

We went out to the van and he seemed to think he would be driving so I let him, as it was fairly obvious that the alarm he had felt at finding human remains had gone. I told him to go into town first so that I could call in at the office and pick up the cheque from the lady from Devon. It wasn't there, and I assumed that she had been so eager to see her daughter that she had changed her mind about detouring through Guildford and had gone straight to London instead. I decided that she would probably have sent it to me in the post. I'm not usually so trusting with people but she had sounded nice. We spent the rest of the day at Birdworld, on the Petersfield road out of Farnham. I can't see what people see in birds myself. They leave me unmoved but they seem to have a relaxing effect on Stanley, not that he seemed to need it, but I was playing for safety.

The weekend came and went and Stanley did what he usually did at week-ends. He took the Transit's engine apart on the Saturday morning and put it back together again by tea-time; when he was through, it ran even more smoothly than it had when he began. On Sunday he tidied up his collection, which meant moving things from one place to another and then back again. A lot of Stanley's time was spent in doing things that didn't really need doing in the first place. I did what I usually did at week-ends, too. I spent most of Saturday in bed and most of Saturday night down at the Cyder House in the village. Sunday was spent in a very similar fashion, varying matters a little by taking the Transit into town and having a drink at the Horse and Groom. The crowd was thin; people, even drinkers, have long memories, and things like IRA bomb attacks tend to make relaxation difficult, even if lightning doesn't often strike the same place twice. Then I went into the Three Pigeons, and decided that the crowd in there was made up of the kind of people I would fight if I was the kind of person who fought in pubs. In the end I drove out to the Squirrel at Hurtmore. I hadn't been in there for a few years, and between visits the brewery's maniacal improvers had been in and removed what had remained of its character. I didn't stay there very long either, and I was back in Shackleford and in bed long before landlords everywhere were calling time. I was quite pleased when Monday morning arrived.

I drove Stanley up to Cobham and spent a few minutes talking to Tommy. He had nothing to add to what I already knew; the police were being very non-committal, but then they usually were. He seemed happy to see Stanley back again, and I gathered that the past few days had seen a number of machines laid low with mechanical faults, and

Stanley's deft and amazing ability with the internal combustion engine was needed.

I drove south towards Guildford, and decided the extra drive up to Cobham and back to Guildford, twice a day, every day, was becoming slightly wearing. I called in at a couple of garages along the way and looked at estate cars, but none fitted the bill too well. I was parking the van in the Quarry when I remembered a second-hand car dealer I had met once or twice when I had been trying to trace some stolen log books for another dealer, who had his own reasons for not reporting the theft to the police. I walked to the office and rang him. He said he didn't have anything in but would look around. He knew about Stanley's ability with engines and I felt reasonably certain he would come up with what I wanted. After I had talked to him I remembered the lady from Devon, and went back to the front door in case I had inadvertently overlooked the cheque. I hadn't; it wasn't there. I went back into the office and rang her. She sounded slightly less enthusiastic than she had before, and I gathered that her daughter had refused to go back to Mummy, and preferred to stay where she was in darkest Battersea, living, in what we used to call sin, with an Algerian wine-waiter from the Park Lane Hilton. I pointed out that her daughter's preferences were no concern of mine, that I had done what I was hired to do, and that a verbal contract was good and binding, and I was sufficiently ungentlemanly to send in the debt collectors if she wasn't forthcoming. She spluttered angrily for several seconds and then told me to expect the cheque the next morning, post office vagaries permitting.

I sat there, glaring at the wall and feeling unjustifiably irritated by it all. I hadn't moved very much when, an hour later the door opened. Some people knock at doors before opening them and some don't. Among those who don't are the police. I think it's lesson three in the training manual, right after 'if you've arrested him he must be guilty' and 'the only difference between criminals and the rest of the public is we haven't caught the others at it yet'. The representative of law and order who clumped heavily into the office was a nasty piece of work I'd met several times before. He was a sergeant in the CID and his name was Norman Fowler, and he hated my guts. We had tangled once when I was representing a client who claimed he'd had a raw deal at an identity parade. I'd proved he had. I'd also proved that he had been guilty anyway by finding something the police had overlooked. Fowler had been in charge of the case. It had given him a reason for hating me, but he would probably have hated me anyway – he was that type. I can usually tolerate policemen; they do the same kind of thing as me except that, unlike me, they can't refuse the dirty and messy jobs and also, unlike me, they don't have to spend good drinking time writing reports for superior officers. Not that I like them; it's a passive state of mind most of the time. Not with Fowler; he was different. He was short, about an inch below my five feet ten, and heavy-set. He wore his dark, thinning hair with a centre-parting that I thought had gone out in the thirties, and he wore suits styled, if that's the word, in the manner of a Second World War demob suit. He should have been about sixty, then he would have looked more or less normal, but he wasn't. He was just thirty and he looked ridiculous. He dropped into the chair on the opposite side of the desk and sneered at me. It was his usual expression.

'Good morning, Sergeant,' I said politely, just to show him that all was well in my world. He ignored the olive branch, and I think I would have been disappointed if he hadn't. He looked round the office and I looked with him, just in case there was a clue to what he was there for. As far as I could see, the carpet was neither cleaner nor more threadbare than usual, the filing cabinets had not suddenly and miraculously been freed from dents and scratches, and there was no sign that the window-cleaner had put me back on his list since I had suggested that giving Christmas boxes to someone who got paid in tax-free cash was slightly superfluous. The Sergeant's gaze eventually returned to me and I smiled patiently at him.

'Come on then, let's go,' he said.

'Where?' I asked, which seemed a reasonable question.

'The Inspector wants to talk to you,' he told me, with all the portentousness his slightly squeaky voice could muster.

'Which Inspector?' I asked.

'Peters.' He bit the name off, but whether it was because he was growing tired of my questions or because of some personal disapproval of his superior, I couldn't guess.

'Why?' I asked. He glared at me for a moment before answering.

'He wants to talk to you and that's all that matters,' he snarled eventually.

'It might be all that matters to you, but I need a better reason for leaving my business unattended,' I told him. He looked around the office again and the sneer spread.

'Business. What business? Now listen Morgan,' he went on without giving me the opportunity of answering, 'you get by in this town because we let you; cross us and you're finished.' I considered telling him to get out and I even thought, fleetingly, of throwing him out, but in the end I did neither. I decided I might just as well go with him. After all, if Inspector Peters really wanted to talk to me, he would, and whether I went to him or stuck out until he came to me, it wouldn't progress the world one little bit. Also there was nothing to be gained by aggravating my relationships with the police, even if Fowler had been wrong when he said they let me survive. But then I didn't really believe that he thought it was true either.

I hadn't met Peters before. In fact I'd never even heard of

him. I soon gathered two things: one was that he was new to the area, and the other was that Fowler really did disapprove of him. He was a tall, gangling, hesitant man, about my age, forty-five or so, but he looked older. His face was thin and tired-looking and his hair had thinned until it barely concealed a pinkish scalp. He looked like anything but a policeman, and he tried to save himself from insignificance by dressing like a man of Fowler's age should have done.

'Very good of you to have come, Mr Morgan,' he greeted me. 'Please sit down.' He waved me into a chair and sat down himself. He glanced up at Fowler as if surprised he was still there. 'Ah, yes, Sergeant. Do find yourself a chair.' There wasn't another one in the office and Fowler barged out and then clattered back in again making rather more fuss than was necessary. When he was finally settled, the Inspector clasped his hands together and leaned forward to rest his chin on them. He beamed at me, contriving to look remarkably like a vicar I once met when I was trying to recover some stolen church plate without causing too many local feathers to fly. It turned out that it was the gravedigger, which meant that scandal was avoided, as he was merely an artisan and not one of the real villagers, who were mostly retired colonels and tea-planters.

'I thought you might like to know what we have found out about the skeleton your cousin dug up,' Peters said. My mind switched into its careful gear. Polite policemen offering information that wasn't really any business of mine smelled like trouble.

'Oh yes,' I said cautiously.

'Yes. We have found out quite a lot, you know.' I didn't but I said nothing. 'Yes,' he went on. 'You see there were other things near where Mr Meadows dug up the body, ah, that is to say, the skeleton.'

'Other things?' I asked, just to show I was listening.

'Yes. There were the remains of a wallet and there were some scraps of clothing and on the body, ah, the skeleton, there was a ring. On one finger – ah, that is to say on the finger bone.'

'Oh,' I said. Peters was silent for a moment while he unclasped his hands and then rearranged them so that this time his fingers made a steeple. He tried to rest his chin on the top but his extended fingers were too high for him, and after scratching his neck unavailingly he carefully resumed his earlier position, and beamed at me once more as if we had come through some great struggle together. I looked sideways at Fowler. The sneer was still there but I couldn't see that it was any different from the one he had used on me.

'Yes,' Peters said suddenly, and I jumped involuntarily. 'The contents of the wallet helped and so did the engraving on the ring. We had to check with our counterparts in New York, but we are fairly sure we know who he is – was.' He managed to make it sound as if he talked to New York every day, and as if they relied on him for help on all their big cases.

'New York,' I said without too much emphasis, but just enough to show that I knew where it was.

'Yes. It seems your cousin has unearthed the last resting place of Michael D'Angelo. The name won't mean anything to you, of course,' he added and I nodded in agreement. It didn't. 'Er, I, well to be frank it didn't mean anything to us either. It seems that D'Angelo was a small-time crook in New York in the 'thirties and early 'forties. He disappeared about 1943 and wasn't seen again.' He paused again and I thought for a moment. It wasn't any of my affair, although I still hadn't worked out why Peters was telling me all this but, as I said before, I have an inquiring mind.

'Disappeared where? Here or New York?'

Peters beamed as if I was his star pupil and had just

proved Einstein's theories to be all wrong. 'New York,' he said. 'Which makes it very interesting doesn't it?'

He was right, it did, but I couldn't get too worked up about it.

'How long has the body been there?' I asked, just to show willing.

'The pathologist can't be too precise, but from various bits and pieces he puts it at between twenty-five and thirty-five years, which could mean that d'Angelo left New York, came straight here and died. Interesting isn't it?' he said again. He seemed very keen to involve me.

'I suppose so,' I said, and then a thought struck me and in spite of myself I asked another question. 'I take it then that the New York police had no record of him having left the country?'

'No,' he said, still proud of me.

'And that was war-time. What about immigration here? They were pretty hot in those days, probably more so even than now.'

'Nothing,' Peters said.

'So, he disappeared in New York over thirty years ago, was never seen again, and now he turns up in a wood in Surrey where he's been lying dead all that time?'

'Yes,' said Peters. 'Fascinating, absolutely fascinating, isn't it, Sergeant?' I was relieved that he had decided to test Fowler's enthusiasm for a change. Fowler sat in his chair, feet planted firmly on the floor, his short squat body looking as if it was tensed ready to bounce up and attack anyone.

'Yes, sir, absolutely fascinating,' he said. The sarcasm in his voice was obvious and I glanced at Peters, but Fowler clearly knew his man well. The Inspector seemed to hear only the words, not the inflection.

'We were wondering,' Peters began again, and the change in his tone told me that we were at last getting to the reason for my presence. 'We were wondering if your cousin had found anything else on the site. Anything that might have a connection that wouldn't be immediately apparent to him, due to his, er, well . . .' He stammered to a stop and I let him suffer. When someone meant only kindness, but didn't have the words to talk about Stanley, I usually helped them out. But Peters, for all his waffling, hadn't brought me there out of concern for Stanley.

'We know about his habit of collecting things,' Fowler put in. 'Has he brought anything home that might be connected?'

'Today was his first day back since he found the skeleton,' I told him.

'I know that,' he said nastily. 'I mean before. Since he's been working on that part of the site.'

'How long would that be?' I asked politely.

'Eh?'

'How long has he been working on that part of the site?'

'I don't know,' he snarled.

'Neither do I,' I told him. He breathed deeply several times, and I was aware that Peters was following the exchange with all the concentration and neck exercise of a spectator at Wimbledon's Centre Court.

'All right,' Fowler said at last. 'During the last three weeks has he brought anything home?'

'He may have done,' I replied. 'I haven't noticed. He certainly hasn't since last week, because I've been collecting him each day. My car was stolen and wrecked,' I added.

'So I heard,' he told me with a lot of feeling. I think he wished it had been me in the wreckage. 'What about before that?'

'I wouldn't have seen anything. He could have brought something in the van. Do you want me to look?'

'Yes please,' Peters put in quickly.

'I'd rather look myself,' Fowler said.

'Get a search warrant and you can,' I told him sweetly. He

muttered something that was almost uncomplimentary and started to get out of his chair.

'That won't be necessary,' Peters said hastily. 'Please have a look and let us know if there is anything that might help.'

'Am I looking for anything in particular?' I asked him.

'No, just anything that seems, well, unusual.'

I nodded and stood up. 'Is that all?'

'Yes, thank you, Mr Morgan,' Peters said, standing up and holding out a hand. We shook hands; his grip was soft and warm, like the vicar's had been. I ignored Fowler as I left and he did the same to me. It was childish but it helped. The alternative would have been to kick him where it would have done most damage.

CHAPTER THREE

I did as Peters asked me, in fact I did it that same day. I felt disinclined to rummage through Stanley's collection when he was there, so I drove straight back to the cottage and went through everything. There was nothing that could have been of any use to anyone, certainly not to Peters. As it was, the exercise left me with a deep depression, as if I had looked into Stanley's mind and found nothing there either. Not that I wasn't aware of the absence of reality there. I was, of course, but most of the time I contrived to pretend it was just one of life's little ironies. It wasn't, it was more like Old Mother Nature at her vicious worst. I sat in the caravan in the middle of the bits of broken furniture, and the old shoes and boots, and thought for the thousandth time about putting Stanley into care and going off to live my own life. I convinced myself that it was the best thing to do, reasoning that I owed myself a life even if it was only for the twenty or so active years I had left. I usually convinced myself of that fact, and I never did anything about it. No, that's not strictly true. Once I did something more; I talked to a psychologist about it. He was a client and I offered to waive my fee for a free consultation. I'm not sure who came off best in the transaction. After the discussion I came away with the clear impression that I was at fault for having so much as thought about dumping Stanley. Eventually I closed up the caravan and went into the cottage and made myself a cup of coffee, and seeing I was there, I spent an hour tidying up the debris that two middle-aged bachelors naturally create. Then I drove the Transit the few hundred yards to the telephone kiosk and rang Peters, and told him there was nothing to interest him. We didn't have a telephone in the cottage; it would have been wasted on me because I only go there to sleep, and not always for that. It would certainly have been wasted on Stanley, because he has never picked up a telephone in his life. It was hot in the telephone box and I felt the need to do something about my depression, so I made another call and talked Julie into letting me drive over.

Julie Matthews is the nearest I've ever come to a steady relationship. She was widowed when her husband tried to shave thirty seconds off the record for his nightly journey home from the City. The A3 in the rush hour isn't the best place to try to do things like that, and he made a nasty mess of several other cars before sliding under the tailboard of a lorry. The tailboard took the top off his neat little family saloon, and with it went Andrew Matthews's head. They wouldn't let her identify the body and I'm not surprised. Julie had been twenty-six when it happened; that was five years ago, and now she augmented her income from her husband's pension scheme by serving as a part-time waitress in various hotels in the district. I used her cold-bloodedly, and after a time she had seemed to see the advantage of that kind of relationship and started to do the same. It had been working that way for two years. I hoped it would last, just so long as it stayed on that particular plane.

She lived in a smallish detached house on a new development at Bramley. Her husband had wanted to be near the golf-course and, as he had been less irresponsible in some things than his motoring technique suggested, there had been sufficient insurance money to pay off the mortgage. So she stayed there in reasonable comfort, with her kids at the local school, and neighbours who baby-sat when she worked, and were sufficiently realistic to look the other way when I made my occasional visits. I suppose it relieved them in a way; as long as there was me, their own husbands weren't at risk.

'Thinking of Stanley again?' she asked. We were lying on top of the bed. It was too hot really – for love-making that is – and we had worked up quite a sweat during the previous twenty minutes.

'Yes,' I said.

'The usual?'

'That's right, the usual.'

'You never will, you know.'

'Maybe not, but it doesn't stop me from thinking about it.'

'You wouldn't know what to do without Stanley,' she said, and I didn't answer, because it sounded like one of those remarks that are too true to bear thinking about. I rolled off the bed and stood up, feeling slightly unsteady. Julie had needed me as much as I had needed her that day. I opened the curtains and looked out at the neat little lawn that looked exactly like all the other neat little lawns in the road, and tried to produce a philosophical thought. I felt the occasion needed one, but I didn't succeed.

'Who cuts your lawn?' I asked instead.

'I do of course,' she said, and behind me I heard her get up and start dressing. I sensed disapproval, but I was a couple of miles away in the Transit before I had worked out what I had said that had caused it. Remarks about lawn-mowing belonged in the same category as questions about the day at the office, and whether little Johnny had said his first words yet. They were too damned domestic; at least they were too domestic for our kind of relationship. I crashed the gears on the van and forced it past a young man in a Triumph Spitfire who couldn't believe his eyes, and I pushed away the thought that, like it or not, the afternoons behind drawn curtains with Julie were numbered. I didn't like it.

The rest of the week went by in a flurry of inactivity. The only real excitement came on the morning after my visit to Julie, when the cheque from the lady in Devon arrived and I walked down to the circular bank at the bottom of North Street and ceremoniously paid it into my account.

Friday was the thirteenth of June and for once the tradition of bad luck was upheld. I dropped Stanley at the site as usual, and then five minutes later found I had a flat tyre. It was on the offside rear and I spent a hair-raising ten minutes changing the wheel, while passing motorists played the game of see-how-close-we-can-go-without-actually-hitting-the-poor-schmuck. I arrived in the office sweaty and dirty, and after washing my hands in the cracked basin in the corner of the room, I picked up the post. Four bills, one written in blood, and a small white envelope from the bank. As far as I knew, I hadn't done anything to incur their wrath, at least nothing unusual, so I opened it. It told me in its pre-printed, quaintly old-fashioned phraseology that the cheque from Devon had bounced. I was still storming up and down, cursing all women, particularly those with straying daughters, when the door was banged open to reveal my friend Sergeant Fowler. He hadn't timed his arrival very well.

'Next time you come in here, knock,' I snarled at him. He seemed unmoved.

'Peters wants you,' he said.

'Peters can piss off,' I told him. 'And so can you.' He stood there, his sneer still in place.

'Would you like to put that in writing?' he asked. I thought of three separate and equally impossible replies to that, but quite suddenly I decided that it was much too hot for arguments, so I walked round him and went out of the office and down the stairs and out into the street. I was halfway to the car park before he caught up with me.

'Where the bloody hell do you think you're going?' he spluttered.

'Nothing to do with you,' I told him without breaking step.

'I told you, Peters wants to see you,' he said.

'I don't want to see him,' I said politely. He grabbed at my arm and pulled me to a stop, his fingers digging into my arm.

'He wants to see you and that's an order,' he announced. I stood looking at him, and with Julie and the bounced cheque still in my mind I decided that Fowler was the last straw.

'Listen to me, you little wart,' I said, still politely, 'no one gives me orders, no one, and that, therefore, includes Peters and, by Christ, it certainly includes you.' He stood hesitating for a moment, then, as it registered that I meant what I said, the sneer slipped a little and was replaced by a look that was almost one of pleasure.

'You're asking for trouble, Morgan,' he told me.

I leaned closer to him and lowered my voice still further. I didn't want witnesses to Morgan's last stand. 'I don't need trouble when people like you are around Fowler. You're not only a blot on the police force, you're a blot on the human race, and if you try to put me out of business or do anything that upsets me in any way, then I give you fair warning, I'll take you apart and afterwards there won't be enough left to feed to the swans on the river.'

He grinned and the sneer came back. 'Try it, Morgan. Just bloody well try it.' I lifted my free hand and took hold of his little finger on the hand that still gripped my arm. I pushed it back and squeezed. The smile faded and with it the sneer. He hung on as long as he could, but I squeezed harder and sweat appeared on his forehead. All around shoppers jostled past without noticing us, and he abruptly released my arm and stepped back. I stepped forward with him, not letting go of his finger.

'I mean it, Fowler,' I whispered, and suddenly I did mean

it. 'Get in my way and, policeman or not, I'll fix you, and what's more I'll make sure every villain in the county hears about it. Then they'll all know you're not the invincible bastard you think you are.' I dropped his hand and turned and walked on up the High Street. Opposite the Grammar School I crossed the road and took the opportunity to glance back. He hadn't moved, and even at a distance of a hundred yards I could see that the sneer was back. He really did think he was invincible.

I walked on up the hill and went into the office of Michael Silver, a solicitor who occasionally gave me odd inquiry jobs. He was in court, and I talked to one of the sexy secretaries he employed to distract the attention of the clients when he presented his accounts. I gave her the address of the lady in Devon, and asked her to tell her boss to write her the standard letter. She gave me the kind of look young girls sometimes give to older men when they think there might just be a bit of life left in the old dog, and I responded with a leer that promised more than I was ever likely to be able to deliver. I told her I would be in the White Horse at lunch time, and she replied with a look that said maybe.

The bar at the White Horse was full of young men and women who looked and acted as if they were about a hundred years younger than I was, and my depression returned in full force. When the girl from the solicitor's office appeared I thought very seriously of sliding out of the rear door, but changed my mind and thought why not? I bought her three large vodka-and-limes in quick succession and then suggested that her boss wouldn't object too strenuously if she took the rest of the afternoon off. She wasn't sure, and I had to invest in another drink before she was in the right frame of mind. I took her back to the cottage, ignoring her outraged expression at having to ride in a van. On the way I stopped at a telephone box and rang Tommy, and told him to lay on some overtime for Stanley in case I was late. At the cottage I was relieved I had done a little tidying up, but even so she turned up her nose a bit. By then it was too late to argue, so I let her understand that she wasn't playing with boys anymore and we went to bed. It was a disaster. I should have known it would be. She didn't fare too badly, however, because I bolstered my reputation by making certain she got something out of it, although on a hot sticky day there are some parts of the female anatomy that are best left alone.

Afterwards I took her home, although she insisted that I dropped her well short of the family residence. It wasn't in one of the best parts of the town, so it was probably fear of being seen in a Transit van that caused her caution. As I drove up the A3 to collect Stanley it started to rain and the temperature dropped quickly by about ten degrees. I let him drive back and sat in the passenger seat, trying to sleep, and trying to rid my nostrils of the smell of two women and one nasty policeman.

While I cooked dinner for us, Stanley repaired the puncture and dried off the van. After we had eaten he disappeared again; he always wax-polished the van after it got wet. I sometimes think he loved that van more than he loved his collection. Or me. It was about ten, and I was thinking of sliding down to the Cyder House for a night-cap, when I heard a car crunch up the drive towards the cottage I opened the door and peered out. The rain had stopped and it was clear and a little chilly. The car was a Cortina and there were two men in it. The driver was Peters. I didn't recognise the other man, but as it wasn't Fowler I wasn't too concerned.

'Good evening, Mr Morgan, I do hope we aren't, er, intruding,' Peters said.

'Come in,' I told him. I led the way into the small living-kitchen, and waved them into hard chairs at the table. I didn't want them to get too comfortable. I looked at the second man. He was big, well over six feet tall and heavy-set. He was balding and he compensated by wearing his hair an inch too long at the back. He looked about fifty and there was about him something that didn't seem quite right. I looked questioningly at Peters. 'Who's your friend?' I asked.

'Oh, er, I'm sorry. This is, er, Sergeant Kusborski,' Peters said. The big man smiled cheerfully and extended a big hand across the table.

'Pleased to make your acquaintance, Mr Morgan,' he said, and the accent was raw American. That explained the not-quite-right look about him. It was the way the shoulders of his jacket were cut, gathered instead of tailored, and the shirt collar had buttons on the points. I should have worked it out without the voice to give it away. Maybe I would have done on any other day but that one.

'Sergeant Kusborski is from America,' Peters said unnecessarily. I wondered about Peters; the hesitancy and the dim remarks were probably an act but he did seem to be taking it too far.

'New York Police Department,' Kusborski added and leaned back in his chair. 'Nice place this,' he said. 'Just how I imagined an English country cottage to be.' I looked round and tried to see it with his eyes. I suppose it did look all right to him: a few oak-beams and a tiled floor, and latch doors all over the place, and the tourists eyes are magically distracted from the cobwebs, the unwashed windows, and the grime on the furniture. 'Needs a woman's touch though,' he added, just to show he wasn't a tourist. I looked at him and he smiled amiably to rob the words of any insult. I go a lot on first impressions. That doesn't mean I trust them, but I do pay heed to them. My first impression of Sergeant Kusborski was that I liked him, and that he was probably honest.

'I take it you're here because of the skeleton?' I asked.

He nodded. 'Yes. Inspector Peters sent a report through, two reports in fact, the first with details about the wallet and the ring that seemed to make it the body of Michael D'Angelo.'

I picked up the implication of the remark. 'You mean it wasn't?'

Kusborski ignored the question, not impolitely; he contrived to give the impression that he wasn't at that point in the story just yet. 'We had no record of the death of D'Angelo, but the file had been marked "missing—presumed dead". I called the cop who had made the note on the file. He's retired now but he remembered making the note. It seems that D'Angelo was small-time but he worked for some of the big boys. Martinez, that's the cop I was telling you about, he knew him, he'd busted him a couple of times. Then, around 1946 or 1947, he was checking on something, and it crossed his mind that he hadn't seen or heard anything about D'Angelo for a long time. So, as he had a tidy mind, he made a few inquiries. He couldn't trace anything after about 1942, maybe early 1943, so seeing that D'Angelo was in a line of business that had a high mortality rate he reckoned there was a good chance he was dead, so he marked the file accordingly.' He paused and looked hard at me.

'So,' I said, aware that I'd had this conversation once with Peters, 'D'Angelo was last heard of in New York, late in '42 or maybe early '43, and now his body is found here, where it's been since about 1943?'

'Yes.'

'And if your friend Martinez has a tidy mind, I assume he checked that D'Angelo hadn't left the country?'

'Not officially.'

'Would it have been easy for him to have left unofficially in those days?'

'Easy enough, with his connections.'

'But it wouldn't have been easy for him to get into this country, not in 1943,' I insisted.

'Maybe not,' Kusborski said in a tone that implied he

didn't think Michael D'Angelo would have had any difficulty in doing anything he had wanted to do. I began to wonder who his connections had been. Kusborski had made two references to them, and I wasn't stupid enough to believe that he had come all the way to England on the thirty-year-old trail of a small-time crook.

'Go on then,' I said.

'I said that Inspector Peters here sent me two reports. The second contained the . . .' He hesitated and turned to Peters for help.

'The coroner's preliminary findings which included a copy of the pathologist's report,' the Inspector put in.

'Yes,' Kusborski went on. 'We checked it against our records. As I said before, D'Angelo had a prison record and his file contained a pretty comprehensive medical description of him.' He paused and I leaned forward in my chair. I didn't know what it all had to do with me, but he certainly had my interest.

'Well?'

'The skeleton was that of a man about five feet eleven inches tall. D'Angelo was five feet five. Additionally, D'Angelo had undergone dental treatment in Ossinging. The details of his teeth were on file and they didn't check either. So, whoever the man your cousin found was, he wasn't Michael D'Angelo.' During the last few seconds Stanley had appeared at the door behind the two policemen. He hadn't made any noise, as usual, and when he spoke both the men sitting opposite me started up out of their chairs.

'There isn't going to be any trouble is there, Harry?' he asked me.

'No, no trouble, Stanley. Is there Inspector?' I said to Peters.

'Er, no,' he said, not very convincingly. Kusborski stood up and held out a hand to Stanley who cautiously took it and shook it and beamed widely at the big American. Kusborski was at least three inches over six feet and there can't have been many times when he had to look up at someone, but he had to with Stanley.

'So you're Stanley,' he said and his voice struck just the right balance of friendliness and authority with no trace of condescension, although I was certain that Peters must have told him all about Stanley and me. Stanley smiled shyly and didn't reply. Kusborski looked at me and then turned away from Stanley and leaned over the table to me.

'Will it upset him to talk about finding the body?' he asked.

'I don't think so,' I said. 'Come and sit with us Stanley.' I waved my hand to his special chair and he pulled it towards the table and joined us, his bright, fixed smile moving from one to the other of our visitors.

'I've been hearing about your collection, Stanley,' Kusborski said, 'Would you show it to me?'

Stanley looked at me and I nodded at him. 'Yes,' he said, 'Would you like to see it now?'

'No, tomorrow will be fine. It's Saturday and I expect you won't be so busy.' Stanley's smile dimmed for a moment.

'Saturday is Stanley's day for working on the van,' I told the policeman. 'Sunday is the day he sorts his collection. That would be better.'

Kusborski nodded and took in Peters's lack of enthusiasm with a quick glance. 'Now we've met I can come alone if that's okay with you, Inspector,' he said.

'Fine with me if that suits Mr Morgan,' Peters said, and contrived to suggest that he didn't much care if it didn't suit me.

'That will be fine, Sergeant,' I told the American. 'Always glad to help the police in any way I can.' Peters looked at me flatly and I smiled mirthlessly at him. The two men stood up to leave and I led the way out of the cottage.

'Thank you Mr Morgan,' Kusborski said. 'I'll see you Sunday.'

'Yes, sure. You know I've looked, don't you?'

'Yes, but I may see things with different eyes.'

'It's a long way to come to look at a pile of junk,' I said.

He smiled at me. 'Maybe,' he said.

'D'Angelo's connections must have been better than even he thought,' I remarked. His smile faded.

'You could say that,' he said and climbed into the Cortina. I stood and watched the tail lights as the car went down the drive. I looked at my watch and decided that if I ran I might just make the Cyder House before eleven o'clock. I ran.

CHAPTER FOUR

Kusborski didn't find anything on his Sunday visit and he looked very thoroughly. I asked him to be as careful as he could with Stanley, and he said he would, and was as good as his word. He let Stanley show him round and he took his time over every exhibit in the collection. After I was sure the American wasn't likely to upset Stanley, I left them to it. I didn't want another trip round the collection. I didn't think my nerves could stand it. It took them most of the morning and by lunch-time Kusborski had given up. I took him down to the Cyder House after assuring him that the name didn't mean they didn't sell other things. He proved to have a very large capacity for whisky, but not so large that he let anything slip about why he regarded the missing D'Angelo, and the unknown skeleton, as so important. We parted on friendly terms and he gave me the address of the precinct where he worked, and told me that if I was ever in New York I should look him up. I told him I would, managing to convey the impression that I crossed the Atlantic every couple of weeks or so.

On the Monday morning my second-hand car dealing friend rang me up to say he had a Volvo estate car that had seen better days and might be just what I was looking for. I collected Stanley from work early that day and he poked around in the engine compartment for a few minutes, and then announced that, unless there was anything really bad inside the crank-case or the gear-box that he wouldn't be able to see until he took it apart, it would do. On the strength of that I bought it, and told the dealer that if we uncovered something terrible we'd bring it back and expect our money back. He looked at Stanley and agreed. Stanley worked on the car every night for a week, and he even forsook the Transit on the following Saturday. On the Sunday morning I had a new motor car. I took it out for a drive. Stanley didn't want to come with me but I insisted. I wish I hadn't.

We got back to the cottage about two in the afternoon. I went into the kitchen to put together some lunch and Stanley went into the out-buildings to start his weekly sorting out of his collection. I hadn't finished washing my hands before I heard him yell. I think the whole village must have heard him. I went out at a run and found him in the first shed by the garage. He was kneeling in the middle of the floor with his arms round a large piece of junk. He was rocking backwards and forwards making a high-pitched keening sound. I reached out and touched his shoulder.

'What is it, Stanley?' I asked. He didn't reply and after a moment I repeated my question. This time he stopped the noise he was making but the swaying motion continued. The third time I asked the question he stopped that too.

'Someone has broken it,' he said.

'Broken what?' I asked.

'Everything,' he said. I looked around the shed. There was a difference. Since the time I'd taken a look through it for Peters everything seemed to have been moved, but Stanley could have done that when Kusborski was there.

'What is broken?' I asked gently. He held up the thing he was holding. It appeared to be the top of a cupboard and there was a jagged break in the wood that looked fresh. I looked round again. This time I noticed there were two upturned paint drums on the floor. They stood about three feet apart and directly beneath a trap-door that led into the loft of the shed. The piece of wood Stanley was holding was about the right length to have formed a platform to let someone pull themselves up into the loft. Provided they were tall enough to have reached, and provided they were heavy enough to have broken the wood when they jumped down again. I brought a step-ladder from the garage and went up into the loft. There were a few odds and ends of Stanley's junk, not many; he preferred keeping his things where he could see them. Stanley seemed to be calmer and I left him while I made a quick tour of the rest of the sheds and the caravan. If I hadn't been looking I wouldn't have seen the slight signs of disturbance. But they were there. Someone had been searching through Stanley's collection. I decided to check the house, and on the way back I collected Stanley and made him sit in the kitchen while I went through the rest of the place. Someone had been through the house as well. He, or probably they – we hadn't been away more than about four hours and Stanley's collection alone would have taken one man more than that period of time – had been good at their job. They'd done it before. And nothing had been taken. They hadn't been thieves. They had been looking for something, and it didn't take a genius to work out that whatever it was that Kusborski wanted, someone else wanted it too.

I went back into the kitchen and made scrambled eggs for us, and tea and a pile of bread and butter and blackcurrant jam, which added together made one of Stanley's favourite meals. When he had eaten his way through it, he had recovered completely, but much as I wanted to go to the office where I could think and telephone, I forced myself to stay at home with him for the rest of the day. I even helped him tidy his collection again.

CHAPTER FIVE

In the morning Stanley didn't comment on the events of the previous day, and neither did I. After breakfast he went off in the Transit, which didn't seem any worse for not having been stripped down and rebuilt that week-end, and I drove slowly down into Guildford and parked the car in the street behind the office. I didn't expect to be there too long. My first call was to the second-hand car dealer who had sold me the Volvo. I told him the car was fine and asked him if he could do me a small favour. He said he could if it was legal, and I said since when had that been a prerequisite of his work, and we laughed and I told him what I wanted. Then I called Tommy Andrews and told him enough about what had happened to get him interested, and to agree to do what I wanted. As soon as I had hung up, the telephone rang. It was Michael Silver, my solicitor friend.

'Do you know who it is you are dunning?' he asked after our preliminary greetings.

'Who?' I asked.

'The woman in Devon of course.'

'Yes,' I said, 'I know she's a woman who owes me money.'

'She is, for God's sake, the widow of a former chief constable.' Silver paused to let the information seep in. 'Did you know?'

'If I had, I would have told you.'

'But you would still have wanted me to write the letter?'

'Yes. Being married to a copper doesn't give her an automatic right to evade payment of bills.'

'Agreed, but there might be better ways of going about it than the way we have.'

'Such as?'

'That's beside the point.'

'You raised the point,' I said.

'For God's sake, Harry, stop quibbling. Okay, so you didn't know and it doesn't make any difference to you. You still want me to chase her for the money?'

'Yes.'

'It's only thirty quid. Less my charges.'

'She owes me the money and she should have paid me. As you said, it's only thirty quid, and thirty quid to her probably means less than it does to me.'

'Okay, I can see you've had a sudden attack of principles. I'll chase her. Do you want to tell me what she hired you to do?' he asked.

'No.'

'I didn't think you would.' He paused. 'Harry, she could make trouble for you. She will have connections that will easily reach from Devon to Surrey.'

'Thanks, Mike,' I said. 'I know you mean well, but do it for me, will you. Unless it will be bad for you.'

'Bad for me? I'll enjoy it.' He laughed and I did too.

'You're as bad as I am,' I told him.

'In some respects,' he said.

'What's that supposed to mean?'

'Little Rosie talks too much,' he said cryptically and hung up. I tried to think who Little Rosie might be but with no success. As far as I knew I didn't know anyone with that name. Five minutes later the telephone rang again and I had my answer.

'This is Rosemary,' the voice said. I tried to place it – she sounded young – and then it registered. The secretary from

Mike Silver's office. I hadn't even bothered to ask her name. I thought rapidly and came to the conclusion that I had nothing to lose by protracting the situation. If that was what she wanted.

'Hello,' I said. 'How are you today?'

'Not as good as the other day,' she said. That surprised me. After all, she hadn't had all that much. But maybe nobody had ever done that to her before.

'Maybe we should do something about that then,' I said.

'When?'

I thought for a moment. 'I'll call you tomorrow,' I said. We talked for a few moments longer and then hung up. I tried to remember her face and I couldn't. I could remember her body though. She must have been at least twenty-five years younger than me. At least. There was a name for men like me. I didn't care to think about it. Instead I thought about Julie. I would have to take care that she didn't find out about Little Rosie. Not that we had any rules of exclusion. We didn't, but she would be unlikely to approve of a relationship with someone that young. It suddenly occurred to me that if my days with Julie were almost over, Little Rosie might make a reasonable stand-in. There *was* a name for men like me. There didn't seem to be very much else for me to do after that, so I sat in my chair with my feet on the desk and tried to think like a detective.

I didn't get very far. All I had was that Stanley had dug up a thirty-year-old body. The body had been planted there with evidence to make it look like a man called Michael D'Angelo, a New York criminal who had disappeared about the same time. That was it, except that there was something somebody wanted. Something that might have been with the body, something that was important enough to bring a New York detective across the Atlantic, and important enough to bring someone else around too. Something they all thought Stanley might have found. And now they all knew he hadn't, they were unlikely to give up and forget it. Whatever it was, it was important. I swung my feet off the desk and dialled the number of the police station. I got through to Peters after a couple of minutes' delay.

'Er, yes?' he said with his usual uncertainty.

'I was wondering if anything had developed?'

'About what?'

'About the skeleton,' I said patiently.

'Er, no,' he said.

'Has your American friend gone home?' I asked.

'Yes,' he said.

'I'm working on a case,' I told him, 'and it involves an American businessman over here, I thought Kusborski might have been able to give me some guidance, but if he's gone, he's gone. I'll do without.'

'You could call him,' he said.

'My clients don't pay the kind of money that allows for international telephone calls,' I said.

'Some of them don't pay at all, by all accounts,' he said.

I took a deep breath. I could see that the old lady in Devon was going to cause me a lot of trouble.

'Oh,' I said, as neutrally as possible.

'Yes,' he said and hung up.

I thought about telling Mike Silver to forget the thirty quid, and then I thought to hell with it and instead I dialled the international operator and asked for the number of Kusborski's precinct. While she was looking it up I tried to work out what the time difference meant. Then I came to the conclusion that it didn't really matter. He probably worked a shift rota of some kind, and my chances of reaching him or not were about equal whatever the time of day or night. I made a note of the number and looked up the dialling code for New York. I got a childish thrill out of dialling the number and an even bigger one when the switch-board operator at the precinct answered. Small things please me. I asked for the Sergeant and was told that it was his day off. I left my name and number and asked the girl to get him to call me when he came in. He called me back within fifteen minutes, which he shouldn't have done if he wanted to pretend that what we were dealing with was a routine matter.

'Harry? It's Ed Kusborski. How're you?'

'Fine,' I told him.

'Something up?'

'Maybe, maybe not. I told him about the search that had been made of Stanley's collection and he was silent for a moment. I listened to the static on the line. Disappointingly, it sounded just like ordinary static on an ordinary inland line.

'It was daylight,' he said eventually.

'Yes.'

'Did any of the neighbours see anything?' he asked.

I stared at the wall and tried to think of an excuse for forgetting to make that most basic of inquiries. 'None I've seen so far,' I told him to save face.

'Well,' he said slowly. 'Keep a sharp eye out, Harry. If you see anyone around or get a whiff of anything you think might be relative, call me. Particularly if you get any descriptions.'

I listened to the static again before I spoke. 'Are you going to tell me what all this is about?' I asked.

There was just static. When he spoke again his voice was low and guarded.

'Not officially,' he said. 'Be at that number this time tomorrow. I'll call you back.' He disconnected the call abruptly. I hung up the receiver and stared at the wall. I came to the conclusion that I was doing that a lot recently. Maybe I'd better buy a picture to hang there, it would make better viewing than the damp patch and the calendar covered with pictures of different types of locks which some security company had sent me.

About four that afternoon I drove back to the cottage. As I climbed out of the Volvo, two slightly-built men in denims and windcheaters materialised out of the rhododendron bushes. One smiled with his teeth while the other hung back, his hands in his pockets, and from the bulge they made he had something else in there apart from his fingers.

'Who are you?' the first one asked.

'Morgan,' I told him. 'I live here.'

The smile moved up into his eyes, but only just. 'Okay. Pass, friend.'

'How many of you are there?' I asked.

'Four,' he said. 'Should be enough.'

'Right. When Stanley comes home, don't show yourself. He isn't to know that you're here. It would worry him.'

'Okay. How do we know which is Stanley?'

'He'll be in a blue Transit van and he's bigger than both of you put together.'

'So I heard,' he said. I nodded and climbed back into the Volvo and went off down the drive. My friend the second-hand dealer seemed to have done what I had asked for.

I stopped the car in the road, climbed out and went to ask my neighbours the questions I should have thought of myself, without help from Kusborski. I didn't get anywhere. I drove further along into the centre of the village and asked the same questions at the little shop by the fork in the road. Nothing there either. I thought about going up to the school, but it had happened on a Sunday and so I didn't bother. I was just about to get back into the car when an old girl I knew by sight came past.

'Hello, Mr Morgan. Nice day,' she said.

'Hello, er, yes it is,' I said, trying to think of her name.

'Did your American friends find you?' she asked.

'Er, no,' I said. 'I was out. They left a note for me though.'

'Oh good. Such polite gentlemen.'

'Yes they are,' I said. 'Both of them.' She nodded and went

on past me. That told me there had been two of them. Unfortunately the way I had played it I couldn't very well ask her for a description. Still, I could always get someone else to ask her.

I reached the site in about half an hour and told Stanley I would be late home. I gave him a five-pound note and told him to buy some fish and chips on his way back to the cottage. That was his second favourite meal and he seemed quite happy about it, and so would the fish and chip shop proprietor. Stanley would boost his takings to record proportions. I put my head into Tommy's door before I left.

'All set?' I asked.

'All set,' he said. 'How many will there be?'

'Maybe none, maybe one, maybe two.'

'Or maybe more?'

'I doubt it.'

'Okay,' he said. 'I'll see you later.'

I went out to the car and drove up the road as far as Esher. I wandered around there for an hour before driving back down to where I could walk to the site without crippling myself, yet far enough away so that the Volvo wouldn't be seen. I found the gap in the wire fence Tommy had left for me, and slipped through. I found a place to sit that gave me as much cover as I needed, and I sat on a folded plastic raincoat I had brought from the car. I didn't want to catch a chill on top of all my other troubles.

As soon as it was dark enough for me to move without being seen, other than from close range, I stood up and eased my cramped muscles. I folded up the plastic raincoat until it was small enough to fit into my pocket, and began to walk through the trees that bordered the excavated path the new motorway would follow. When I reached a point that was within two hundred yards of where Stanley had uncovered the skeleton, I stopped and dropped into a crouch. I wriggled into a reasonably comfortable position against the bole of a tree and wished it was August instead of June. It was turning cold. It was even colder before I heard them.

They weren't being too careful, which surprised me at first. Then I realised they had no reason to expect they were being observed. Still, they should have been more cautious. There were two of them and they passed quite close to me, close enough for me to hear the voice of the one doing the talking, but not close enough for me to hear the words. The voice seemed to have an American accent but that could have been wishful thinking on my part. Just past where I crouched they stopped and began to move slowly, quartering the ground carefully in the light of the powerful torches they carried. As far as I could see they were of medium height and slim, and dressed in dark trousers and jackets. No overcoats, so they were not planning on staying for long. As far as I could see, they were not carrying spades or anything else with which to dig. Altogether they were not behaving as efficiently as I had somehow expected them to. It was about an hour and a half before they gave up and went back the way they had come. I listened carefully and eventually I heard an engine start and a vehicle drive off. Seconds later I heard another engine start up and I grinned to myself. Tommy was doing his part of the night's work. Then I heard a third engine start and the smile left my face. I hadn't allowed for that in my calculations. I hadn't allowed for that at all.

I drove back to the office, worrying about Tommy. It wasn't his affair and I was concerned that he might be in trouble. Come to that, it wasn't my affair either. I was just interfering. Interfering in something I knew nothing about but which had aroused my curiosity and, I have to admit, irritated me. I don't like my home being searched. It was after midnight when the telephone rang. It was Tommy and I breathed a sigh of relief.

'I thought you said there wouldn't be more than two of them,' he said.

'I heard the third car,' I said. 'It had me worried.'

'It had me bloody worried too,' he said. 'Anyway, the third car you heard was mine. The two who came on to the site walked in from the north, so I backtracked to find their car. When I did I went over to have a look inside, then I spotted someone else doing the same thing, so I stayed where I was, and when he went off I followed him. He was with another man and their car was a few yards farther up the road.'

'So what happened?' I asked.

'I went back to the site entrance and waited. When your friends came back I watched them go up to their car. I took a chance they would come back towards me. It wouldn't have mattered if they hadn't; I'd taken the car number. Anyway they did come back this way. A few seconds later the second car came by. I'd taken their number as well. I followed on.'

'Good man, Tommy. If you ever need a job . . .' I let the remark hang in the air. He knew it was my way of paying him a compliment.

'Balls,' he said amiably.

'Where did they go?'

'The man and the woman . . .'

'Woman?' I interrupted.

'The two that came on to the site. One was a man, the other was a woman. Didn't you see that?'

'I wasn't close enough,' I said.

'Yes, well, one of them was a woman.'

'Okay, go on, Tommy. Where did they go?'

'They went to Thatchers Hotel at East Horsley, the man and the woman. The second car seemed to be doing what I was, just checking. They only stayed there a moment; they didn't get out. Then they went off again. I reckoned there was nothing to be gained by staying there so I followed them.'

'Good man. Where did they go?' There was a pause before he answered. He sounded less happy than before.

'Sorry, Harry, I lost them.'

'No matter, Tommy. It happens to the best of us.' I thought about it for a moment. 'Where were they heading?'

'They went on past Thatchers towards Leatherhead. I was behind them for the first couple of miles, and then they, well, they just disappeared. No trace. I drove up and down a few times in case I could spot where they might have turned, but no luck. There are a few roads along there and there are plenty of houses they could have turned into.'

'Yes, okay, Tommy. Thanks a lot. You're a good mate.'

'Yes, so you tell me, when it suits you. Are you going to tell me what all this is about?'

'If I knew I would.'

'I'll believe you.'

'True, Tommy.'

'Okay, Harry. See you.' We hung up and I looked at the damp patch on the wall. I found myself wondering why the warm weather hadn't dried it out. I really would have to get a picture to put up.

I drove back to the cottage, and as I parked the Volvo one of the four men I'd hired floated up out of the darkness.

'It's me,' I said.

'Yeah, okay, chief. You back for the night?'

'Yes. Thanks. You can push off now. I'll ring when I'm going to be out again.'

'Right.' He paused as if he wanted to add something else. 'Big fellow your mate.'

'Yes he is.'

'I would have thought he could look after himself,' he said.

'Things aren't always what they seem,' I said. He nodded

in the darkness and floated off again. I heard him whistle softly and a moment later I saw his partners materialise out of the gloom, and the four of them walked swiftly and silently out of the drive. I felt slightly less safe after they had gone and wondered for a moment if I would have been wiser to have kept them there all night. If I had I might have slept easier. As it was I didn't sleep at all, at least not until it was starting to get light.

CHAPTER SIX

The following morning I drove to the office and called Julie. We talked casually for a few minutes and we made a tentative date for the following afternoon, crime and other things permitting. Then I asked her if she knew anyone at the Thatchers I could approach. She thought for a moment and gave me the name of an assistant chef who might not be averse to earning a few pounds on the side. The assistant chef turned out to be a slightly-built individual who looked remarkably under-fed for someone in his line of work. I told him what I wanted to know, and he said it wouldn't do for hotel staff to give away information about guests, and I told him he was quite right, but if the guests turned out to be undesirable he would have done his employers a great service, and he would have been paid for it as well. He agreed with me, whether at the thought of doing a service for his employers or of being paid for it, I wasn't sure. He disappeared for about ten minutes, presumably to talk to someone who knew what I wanted to know. He gave me names and information and told me they were sitting in the hotel's lounge. I gave him some money and he slipped it out of sight with all the speed and practice of someone who'd done it before. I walked through the kitchen and into the lounge. There were quite a few people in there, but I spotted my two easily enough. I walked straight through the room and out again. I had seen what I wanted to see.

I drove back to Guildford and went up to the office.

I killed time waiting for the call Ed Kusborski had promised me, and I was immersed in the crossword puzzle in the *Daily Mail* when his call came through.

'Are you alone?' he asked me.

'Yes,' I told him, thinking maybe American policemen did behave the way the movies claimed.

'I'm calling from home,' he said. 'Not that this is unofficial; it's just that it's delicate. The fewer people who know about it, the fewer leaks there will be.'

'Quite a few people seem to know about it already,' I told him.

'Why, what's happened?' he asked urgently.

'I'll tell you later,' I said. 'You tell your bit first.'

'Okay,' he said reluctantly. 'We're interested in the skeleton Stanley found because of the link with Michael D'Angelo. Even if it isn't him, there's enough evidence to show that he is involved, and as he's been missing since that body was buried he might be there too. Buried somewhere in the same area.'

'And that's what you were looking for?'

'Yes.' Kusborski didn't sound very convincing.

'You didn't expect to find another skeleton when you searched Stanley's collection?' I said.

'True, that isn't what I was looking for.'

'What were you looking for?' I asked.

'I don't know, Harry, truly I don't. I just hoped there might be something that would help.'

'Help do what?' I asked. I heard what sounded remarkably like a sigh mixed in with the static.

'Okay,' he said. 'I guess I'll have to tell you.'

'It will help me know who I'm up against,' I said. There was a long pause.

'That's the second time you've hinted that something's going on over there. You'd better tell me, Harry.'

I nodded to myself. Maybe he was right. 'Someone else is taking an interest,' I said. I told him about the events of the night before and how Tommy had trailed both cars.

'Did he get a description?' he asked.

'I have a description of two of them,' I said, 'and their names.'

'Great. Go ahead.'

'There was a man and a woman.' I told him. 'The woman is in her late twenties, tall, slim, very blonde hair, grey eyes, high cheek-bones. She's registered as Selena Cantrell. The man is in his mid-thirties, long face, heavy chin – craggy would be a good word for him. Dresses like a banker. Registered as John Mason. Both have American accents, passports, luggage and clothes. Gave separate addresses in New York. They are booked into separate rooms and as far as the staff know they really are sleeping that way, although they dine together.'

'They will be,' Kusborski said. 'Sleeping apart I mean.'

'You know them?' I asked unnecessarily.

'I know of them,' he said. 'What about the other two?'

'No description yet, but someone in the village saw the visitors I told you about. All she told me was that they were men, so I'm fairly certain they were the two in the second car.'

'I think we ought to know who they are,' he said. 'Quickly.'

'I think something else ought to happen quickly,' I told him.

'What?'

'It's time I knew what I'm involved in.'

'You're right, Harry. Can you be patient?'

'How patient?'

'Forty-eight hours patient.'

'Maybe. What happens in forty-eight hours?'

'That's when I'll be knocking on your door, Harry.'

'I can hardly wait,' I told him and hung up. Forty-eight hours seemed a long time to wait, and with only the old girl in the village to talk to I decided to have another run out to East Horsley, to see if I could pick up anything on the other two men. I was half-way down the office stairs when I remembered that Tommy said he'd taken the registration numbers of the two cars. And I was supposed to be a detective. I went back up the stairs and rang him. He gave me the numbers and I hung up quickly before he could ask me any other questions I wouldn't be able to answer. I telephoned a friend of mine in the licensing department at Tolworth Tower. He told me that the computer in Swansea had taken charge but he thought he might be able to help. He called me back in twenty minutes and told me that the car I was interested in was a Hertz rental Ford Granada. I rang Hertz and got precisely nowhere. I thought about calling Peters but I came to the conclusion that it would be better if I waited to see if Kusborski wanted the local police involved. That gave me the rest of the day to fill in so I called Julie. She was on her way out to work so I called Little Rosie instead. Well, what would you have done?

CHAPTER SEVEN

As it turned out, that wasn't such a bad idea after all. Calling Rosemary I mean. Although my performance was only marginally better than the first time, she seemed to have an insatiable appetite for the kind of thing I was prepared to do to her. Quite clearly no one else had got around to doing it before me. Mind you, the age gap showed. She could have gone on long into the night if I had let her, or, to be a little more precise, if I had been able to keep it up into the night. As it was, I called a halt in the late afternoon and dressed quickly while she was in the bathroom. When she came back into the bedroom she wrinkled her nose in mild irritation at my fully dressed state and slowly began to dress too. I stood and watched her and the reverse striptease proved to be just the erotic stimulant she clearly meant it to be, but I did nothing about it. There wasn't enough time before Stanley came home, and the memory of that other time he had lost control was too clear in my mind to risk having a randy young girl on the premises.

As I drove out of the village I saw the old girl who had seen my visitors, and I stopped and thought quickly. For some reason I felt unwilling to ask her directly; I had already said that I knew them and to reverse that by asking for a description might raise doubts in her mind. I couldn't see that such a thing would cause me any problems, but you never know. I hastily concocted a tale for Rosemary, and as she hopped out of the car to talk to the old lady I walked back to the little shop-cum-post-office and bought some stamps I didn't need.

When I got back to the Volvo, Rosemary was already there.

'Okay?' I asked.

'Yes, I've got a description of them, and the old lady thinks I'm your secretary and I'm going to meet them in London.'

'Good. She didn't think it odd that I hadn't described them to you myself?'

'No. I told her you'd only corresponded with them, never met them.'

'Good girl,' I said.

'Am I?'

'What?'

'A good girl?'

I looked at her. She was sitting straight-backed in her seat. Her mid-brown hair hung straight from her centre-parting, and covered most of her face so that I couldn't see her expression. I wasn't too sure where the conversation was leading and I was completely unsure of the kind of answer she wanted.

'In a manner of speaking,' I said lightly. She made a noise that sounded like a delicate snort of exasperation. Obviously my answer hadn't been the one she wanted. She didn't speak to me all the way into town, and when I stopped near to her home she sat silent for a moment.

'Take me up to the door,' she said eventually. 'It's the house with the blue paintwork down there.' I started up again and moved the fifty yards to her door. Perhaps I had been right that first time; perhaps it had been the van she didn't want to be seen in rather than me she didn't want to be seen with. She made no attempt to get out of the car, but sat there silently for several minutes during which I tried to think of something to say that would break through the wall that had suddenly appeared between us. Then I wondered if I wanted the wall to be broken. Maybe a quick break now was the best thing. After all, she was a lot younger than me.

'How old are you?' I asked abruptly.

'What's that got to do with it?' she asked.

'Good question, but I asked mine first.'

'Nineteen.' Christ, I thought, twenty-six years younger than me. A break was definitely the best thing that could happen. She opened the door and climbed out and stood on the pavement. I put the car in gear and waited for her to walk away. She stopped and looked in through the open window.

'You don't care at all, do you?' she said. 'You don't care that I love you?' She turned and ran up the path and through the blue front door. I stared at it for a few moments after it had closed and then drove away. I didn't believe her of course. Two meetings, admittedly extremely intimate ones, aren't enough to justify a declaration of love. Some young women of that age are mature, a damned sight more mature than women of nineteen were when I was that age. Unfortunately for me, Little Rosie seemed to be one of the immature ones.

By the time I reached home again Stanley had arrived, and I kept my feeling of irritation in check; after all it wasn't his fault that I had a disorganised sex life. After I had made a meal for us I went down to the telephone box in the village and rang the second-hand car dealer, and ordered up the troops. They arrived about eight o'clock, while Stanley was watching television. I told them I would be back about midnight or just after, and they dissolved into the darkening garden.

I was at Thatchers in about half an hour. The man and woman who had visited the site were in the dining-room. There was no sign of the others and the Granada wasn't anywhere in evidence. I drove on up the road towards Leatherhead, looking into all the drive entrances and turnings off the main road. It was a hopeless task, of course, and I rapidly tired of it. I turned back towards Guildford, and on the way there I decided to go up to the site on the offchance the two men in the Granada might be there. I turned into Ockham Road just past Thatchers, and that was when I discovered that I had acquired a tail. I watched the car carefully in my rear-view mirror, but it was too far off, and with its headlights full on I was unable to see what make of car it was. I turned off at Ockham and went through Martyr's Green just to make sure I wasn't developing a persecution complex. The car followed me, and so when I reached Cobham, instead of turning towards the main road, I turned right and drove down to Stoke D'Abernon and pulled into the car park of the Running Mare. I ordered a half pint of bitter in the bar and sat against the wall so that I could see the back and front doors, and waited to see what happened.

Nothing did, and after I had spun the half pint out for about forty minutes, I went back out to the car. On the way I checked all the other cars in the car park and in the road outside. There was one Granada, but when I drove off it didn't follow me. A dark blue Marina saloon did. I drove on to the A3 and turned north towards London. Where the road passed through Claremont Woods, I pulled into the car park and killed the lights, and was out of the car and among the trees before the Marina reached me. I stayed motionless in the trees while the driver of the Marina made up his mind what to do. He had probably guessed that I had seen him and he made no attempt to get out of the car. Instead he turned off his lights so that I stood no chance of seeing him in reflected light, or of seeing his number, and then he spun the wheel and went out of the car park and out on to the road heading south. He was some distance away before he switched on his lights. I ran for the Volvo and went after him. I had him well in sight and was closing in on him rapidly in an attempt to read his number plate – there seemed no point in pretending I wasn't there – when the police car appeared out of nowhere, as they usually do, and overtook me before flagging me down. They were very polite and also very young. One of them seemed no older than Rosemary. They were also very thorough. They checked the car from top to bottom, they checked my papers and they checked me. They even breathalysed me, although I wasn't sure they were entitled to do that. I didn't argue. The more checks they made, the longer they took, the more certain I became of the identity of the driver of the Marina.

The following day I proved my guess. I sat outside the police station watching cars come and go for an hour before Sergeant Fowler arrived. He was in a dark blue Marina. I thought about things for a while and decided that my decision to remain patient until Kusborski arrived was still my best course of action. The less I did, until I knew what was going on, the better. Anyway I still had a living to earn.

I walked up one side of the High Street and back down the other, calling in all the insurance offices and all the solicitors' offices. All except Mike Silver's that is. His office was now off limits to me, at least until I decided what to do about Rosemary. It took most of the day; there are a lot of insurance company offices and a lot of solicitors in Guildford. By the end of the day I was tired and fed up. I hadn't picked up any work either. I went back to the office and looked at the damp patch and thought about going out to buy the picture to cover it. Then I thought of a better way to deal with the problem. I spent half an hour rearranging the furniture so that I looked at a different wall, one without a damp patch. I don't know why I hadn't thought of that before.

I was pleased when it was time for the pubs to open.

CHAPTER EIGHT

Kusborski arrived on time. He came into the office making it seem small and crowded, and it crossed my mind that in all the time I had been there Stanley had never come up to the office. But then I had never asked him if he wanted to. It had never occurred to me that he might like to visit the place where I worked. Kusborski settled himself in my other chair and I poured out a generous measure of Scotch from the bottle I had bought especially for the occasion. I made a mental note that if after the talk we were about to have I couldn't see any money in it for me I would bow out before I went broke. The American policeman must have been reading my mind.

'Before I begin,' he said. 'What's going to be in this for you?' The question wasn't one I could answer so I said nothing. 'I'm here with the permission of the English police,' Kusborski continued.

'Peters,' I said ignoring the apparent *non sequitur*.

'A hell of a way farther up the ladder than him,' he said. 'Now, the English police can't pay you, and neither can the NYPD.' I waited. 'And I certainly can't,' he added. That seemed to rule everyone out. It didn't look as if I was going to stay involved after all. 'There just might be a way for you to stay involved,' he went on. 'I plan to be here for about ten days. If it takes that long to explore all the angles, that is. I'm being paid expenses and if I stay with you and use your car I can legitimately pay you. It won't be much but it will be better than nothing, and quite frankly it would help me.'

I looked at him curiously. 'How?' I asked.

'Local knowledge, connections.'

'The police have all those and more besides.'

'Maybe, but they also have rules of procedure, rules that might be more problem than help.' He looked at me carefully for a moment. 'Also you are less likely to get upset if I have to bend a few heads.'

'For instance?' I asked.

'No one in particular,' he said. 'But, with the kind of people we're dealing with, that could prove to be the kind of language they'll understand best.'

'About that,' I said, 'I was promised an explanation.'

He grinned at me. 'Yes, sorry about that, Harry. Before I tell you what it's all about there's the matter of the two guys who searched your house. Did you get a description of them?'

'Yes. One of them is of medium height and stocky build, dark complexion and beaky nose. The other tall, thin and good-looking, also dark.' He nodded. 'Mean anything?' I asked.

'Could be. The first one certainly, and the second one could fit . . .' his voice trailed off. 'I'd better start at the beginning,' he said. I topped up his drink and waited. 'Does the name Capelli mean anything to you?' he asked.

'Capelli? Joe Capelli?'

'That's the one,' he said.

'Yes. A big man in the rackets before the war. Friend of Capone.'

'In a manner of speaking. In fact Guiseppi Capelli was for New York what Capone was for Chicago. Only Capelli was a little more careful. He never saw the inside of a prison and he never caught unmentionable diseases either.' Kusborski grinned. 'Old Joe was a real family man. He loved his wife and he gave all his children good educations. He saw that his three daughters made good marriages, outside the rackets, and, when he knew he was dying, he made certain there would be no feuds after the funeral. Feuds that would split the organisation down the middle. He believed in the organisation, it was as much his family as his real family. And he wanted it to survive. So, when he knew he was going to die – he had cancer of the throat – he called a meeting and he handed over the running of the organisation to Fiore Gizzo. Gizzo was about fifty at the time and that was Capelli's idea of the right age for the job. He wanted Gizzo to run things for the next fifteen or twenty years and then hand over to one or more of Capelli's sons, who by then would be old enough for the job. He had three sons. Giorgio, the eldest, was thirty when the old man died, Franco was twenty-three, and Antonio was two years younger than that. Now, old Joe Capelli was a lot of things, most of them bad, but he wasn't a fool. He knew that there was always a possibility that when the time came for Gizzo to hand over he might have other ideas about who should succeed him, and he knew that even if Gizzo played it straight there might be other factors that would be in the way of the boys. So he made arrangements for his personal fortune to be left to the three of them, and that's where things started to go wrong.'

'How?'

'I have to admit I don't know,' Kusborski answered. 'All I do know is that none of the brothers ever got the old man's fortune. At least that's the story and there's no evidence to suggest that isn't true.'

'What happened to Gizzo?' I asked.

'Nothing happened to him. He's still alive and still running things. He's well past eighty now and he shows no signs of giving in. But he must die one day and that day has to be getting close.'

'What about the brothers?'

'George and Frank are still working for the organisation. They each run parts of the city under orders from Gizzo. They both hate his guts and they're waiting like vultures for him to go. If they were half the men their father was they'd have done something about it by now.'

'And the other brother?'

Kusborski picked up the glass and drained it. I refilled it in silence. I hoped his expense account was big enough to accommodate his capacity for booze.

'Tony was drafted a week after the old man died. That was in December 1942. He went into the army, spent a few weeks at a training camp in upstate New York, and then he came here.'

'Here? To England?'

'Yes. And not just to England. He came right here to Surrey. He was posted to one of your army camps at a place called Pirbright? You know it?'

'Yes, of course. It's no distance at all from here. There are several camps there, mostly Guards depôts.'

'That's the place,' Kusborski said. 'You see Tony volunteered for a special unit that was being trained to go into Italy as an advance force before the invasion. The unit were all Italian-Americans, all fluent in the language and all, because of their descent, looking the part. Obviously it was easier for our people to produce a group like that than it would have been for the British Army.'

'Yes, but . . .'

'Go on. Ask the question.'

'I was just wondering why he volunteered for that kind of thing, and for that matter why it was he didn't get out of going into the army at all. Maybe I've seen too many movies, but I would have thought he would have been able to dodge the draft.'

Kusborski nodded slowly and smiled. 'You asked the right question. Our people asked it then, and, what's more, his own brothers asked the question too. And nobody's ever been able to answer it.'

'Why? What happened to Tony?'

'He was killed in a plane crash.'

'Where?'

'Here. An airstrip at a place called Dunsfold. The plane crashed on take-off. Almost everyone on board was killed. There were five survivors. Tony wasn't one of them.'

'Okay,' I said. 'I'm with you up to now, but I can't see the connection with what's been going on here.'

'That's because I haven't got to that part yet. The skeleton that your cousin found. The papers and other bits and pieces led us to think at first that it was a man called Michael D'Angelo. Forget for the moment we know it wasn't him. D'Angelo was in his early twenties at the time he disappeared. He was a button man in the organisation and he was a friend of the Capelli brothers, particularly of Frank and Tony. So, there's the first question: was he here? And if he was, where is he now? The next question is more interesting: who is the dead man?'

I thought for a moment. 'Tony Capelli?' I said slowly.

Kusborski nodded. 'A very real possibility,' he said.

'Why are the NYPD interested in all this?' I asked.

'Various reasons,' he said. 'Chiefly, when Gizzo dies all hell is likely to break loose. It might give us an edge if we had something to hang on the Capelli brothers.'

'You think they had something to do with the skeleton being buried there?'

'Someone did.'

'Tell me,' I said. 'You've seen the pathologist's report. What did the skeleton, Mr Bones, what did he die of?'

He grinned at me. 'Good name,' he said. 'Mr Bones had no marks to suggest how he died. No broken bones, no blows to the skull, no scratches on the ribs a knife might have made. No chips off bones that could have been made by a bullet.

For all the pathologist knows he could have died from natural causes.'

'Okay,' I said. 'Tell me about all these people that are running around here now.' Kusborski reached into the inside pocket of his jacket and brought out a sheaf of papers. He selected two and pushed them across the desk to me. Both had photographs attached, although neither was a posed police shot. I looked at them and recognised them both.

'Recognise them?'

I nodded and read the information on the sheets. Their names, Selena Cantrell and John Mason, were real. Neither had any aliases listed. The woman was described as a secretary and the man as a lawyer. The name of George Capelli appeared on both sheets. They both worked for him: the woman was his personal secretary, the man was his attorney.

'Yes,' I said eventually. 'No doubt they're the two. And they both work for George Capelli?'

'In a manner of speaking.'

'What does that mean?'

'Selena Cantrell is George's mistress. His wife died a few years back and he has no children. She's the only person close to him. As far as we know he trusts her and she doesn't seem to have done anything to abuse that trust.'

'There's a big age gap,' I glanced at the sheet. 'She's twenty-seven and he's . . . how old?'

'Sixty-four. It doesn't necessarily mean anything. Some women prefer older men.'

I nodded, thinking to myself that he was right, and wondering if George Capelli had felt the way I felt with Rosemary.

'What about the man, Mason?' I asked.

'Genuine lawyer, handles the legitimate side of Capelli's business. Never touches the dirty end.'

'But he knows about it?'

'Of course.'

'That raises an interesting question; why would he send his girl friend and his clean lawyer?'

'Exactly what I was wondering.'

'What about the other two?' I asked.

Kusborski sorted through more of the papers and fished out two of them. This time they were photocopies of police file sheets. He pushed them across to me.

'I made a list of the men we hadn't seen around for a few days', he said. Checked with the airlines and ended up with a short-list of those who might be over here. These two come closest to the descriptions you gave me earlier.'

I looked at the sheets. 'Can I borrow these?' I asked.

'Yes.' He hesitated for a moment. 'If they are the ones, then they can give us trouble. Alda is bad enough; three unprovable homicides against him. As for Martinelli, he makes the rest of his crowd look like juvenile offenders.'

'Who are they working for? Gizzo?' I asked.

Kusborski shook his head. 'No, that's what's bothering me. As far as I can see, Gizzo isn't involved in this. Alda and Martinelli are Frank Capelli's boys.'

'So it's brother against brother?'

'Looks that way. Seems that blood isn't always thicker than water.'

I looked at him for a moment. 'Some people have all the luck,' I said and regretted it immediately.

'Let's find out about the two men,' he said.

'Okay,' I said.

We went down the stairs and I took Kusborski to Shackleford and introduced him to the old lady. I decided to risk looking stupid and told her that the two men she had seen were not really friends of mine, and would she mind looking at some photographs and identifying them for me. The old girl cottoned on fast. After all, she knew I was a detective, or was supposed to be one.

'Are they criminals, Mr Morgan?' she asked eagerly.

I glanced at Kusborski and he nodded his head.

'Yes,' I said, adding hastily and unjustifiably, 'there's no danger though.' She didn't seem concerned at the prospect of tangling with criminals, however – too much television I suppose. Everyone knows bullets don't hurt; after all, the guys who get shot are there next week as if nothing had happened.

She glanced through the wad of papers Kusborski handed her. They were all the papers he had in his pockets. She picked out two and hesitated over a third. Then she shook her head and handed the two to me. She had picked out Alda and Martinelli. I glanced at the one she had hesitated over. It was of the girl. I wondered if Kusborski had left that one in the pile deliberately. I turned it over in my hands.

'Do you know her?' I asked the old lady.

'I'm not certain, dear,' she said. 'It's just that, well, there was someone in the post office this morning. Would she have an American accent too?'

I looked at Kusborski and we read one another's minds, and we ran for the car with barely a good-bye to the startled old girl.

'Straight up to the house?' I asked.

He thought for a moment and then nodded. 'Yes. They're not like Frank's boys. They won't give us any trouble, and we're more likely to get something out of them than we are out of anyone else.'

I spun the wheel and we went up the drive to the cottage with a spray of gravel shooting out behind us.

They were in the caravan and they didn't offer any resistance. They didn't say anything either. We took them into the cottage and sat them side by side on the slightly battered settee. It sagged in the middle where Stanley sat on it to watch television. Kusborski started.

'What are you looking for?' he asked them. Neither of them answered. I looked at the woman. It didn't cause me any pain. Close to, she was more than merely attractive; she was beautiful. Her skin had a satin-like appearance that made me want to touch it, not out of lust but just to see if it felt as soft as it looked. Her eyes were not really the grey I had thought them to be; they were a very pale green with tiny flecks of brown in them. I could have looked at her all day. She let her glance drift across Kusborski's face and on to mine. It lingered for a second and there was nothing in her expression to suggest that she saw anything worth coming back to for a second glance. Maybe I was stuck with the Rosemarys of this world after all.

Kusborski leaned over them. From behind he looked menacing. If I'd been where they were I think I would have been frightened to death.

'I asked a question,' he said, 'and I think it's one you should answer. Particularly you, Mr Attorney.' He stuck a finger into Mason's chest and I heard the sudden exhalation of breath quite clearly. Mason looked at the woman and she nodded imperceptibly. That showed who was boss.

'Nothing specific, Sergeant,' he said. 'We heard about the skeleton being found, and that it had been rigged to suggest it was Mike D'Angelo's. We wanted to be certain nothing had been overlooked.'

'Such as?' Kusborski added.

'Oh, papers, anything that might give us a clue to who the dead man was and what might have happened to D'Angelo.'

No one spoke for several minutes and I wondered why the lawyer and the girl were feeding us such a weak story. Maybe they thought we were simple-minded. I remembered about Stanley as I thought that. His habit of collecting odds and ends of rubbish was becoming extraordinarily well known in many far-flung places. I wondered who was behind the free exchange of information that seemed to be taking place.

'What do you think happened to D'Angelo?' Kusborski asked.

'I haven't an idea,' Mason answered.

Kusborski turned to the woman. 'What about you, Miss Cantrell. Have you any ideas you would like to share with us?'

She turned her eyes on to the big policeman. 'None at all,' she said. Her voice matched the rest of her. Slightly husky and soft, with one of those pleasant American accents that come from having all the nasal twangs of the big cities rubbed off them. 'I must ask you a question as well, Sergeant. What jurisdiction have you here? What authority have you to ask us questions?' She looked at Kusborski levelly.

'None,' he said and laughed without humour. 'Don't get ideas, Miss Cantrell. I'm here with the knowledge and consent of the British police, and they'll ask the questions for me if that's the way you want it.'

'What right have they to ask us questions?' she asked.

'What right?' Kusborski growled, 'the right of any police force anywhere when someone is found on private property without the knowledge and consent of the owner.'

Her eyes turned to me and somewhere in their depths I thought I saw a smile; at least there was more expression than there had been before.

'Always provided Mr Morgan lays charges,' she said.

'He will,' Kusborski said flatly.

The eyes warmed up fractionally. 'Will he?' she said softly, as if to herself.

Kusborski turned to me, and when he was sure the others couldn't see him he smiled broadly and winked. 'He'll do as I tell him,' he snarled in complete contrast to the expression on his face.

'Like hell I will,' I said, taking what I assumed was the line he wanted me to take. The smile spread still further to show I had said the right thing.

'You'll do as I say,' he bellowed.

'Go to hell,' I yelled back trying to work out the name of the game we were playing. His face suddenly hardened and he spun round on the woman.

'So you've got to him as well, have you?' he ground out. 'How much are you paying him? The same rate as the guy who washes your car, or is he worth as much as the man that empties your trash?' Without waiting for a reply he turned on his heel and stormed out of the room. It wasn't a bad exit. There was silence in the room and we sat listening to his feet crunching down the gravel drive towards the road. I waited for one of my visitors to speak. I didn't have anything to say anyway. It was the man who spoke first.

'What was all that about?' he asked the girl.

'Ask Mr Morgan,' she said. They both looked at me. I looked at the man for a moment. He seemed genuinely not to know. I turned to the girl. The smile was more in evidence in her eyes.

'I had the impression I was being hired,' I said.

She nodded gently and a wisp of her very blond hair fell over her forehead. It made her look even younger and even more attractive. I was beginning to worry about that when she spoke.

'Are you for hire?' she asked.

'Nobody else has hired me in this case,' I said.

'Who else is there to hire you?' Mason asked, his voice tense. He was sharp, very sharp.

'Alda and Martinelli,' I said.

There was no doubt I had told them something they didn't already know.

'They're here?' the lawyer snapped.

I nodded and looked at the girl. 'Are you hiring me?' I asked her.

She nodded. 'Yes.'

'To do what?'

'Help us find what we're looking for.'

'What's that?'

She shook her head in a slightly lost gesture. 'We don't really know,' she said. I was watching her eyes and they were fixed on mine. If I read them right, she did know what they were looking for; only Mason didn't.

'That won't make life very easy,' I said lightly.

'We'll know when we find it,' Mason put in.

'That will help a lot,' I said coldly. I thought it was time to shake them up.

'You haven't found it here,' I said, 'and you didn't find it two nights ago on the site.' Their eyes met. 'Are you comfortable at the Thatchers?' I asked. Mason looked at me as if he would have liked to step on me. The first signs of a real smile touched the woman's mouth.

'I think we may have been a little too careless, John,' she murmured. Then her voice changed. 'Wait in the car,' she said brusquely. Mason glared at her, two spots of bright colour burning on his cheeks. He pushed himself up out of the settee and walked stiff-legged out of the room.

I waited until I heard his footsteps fade down the drive. I wondered fleetingly where Kusborski was hiding, and that made me think of something else too.

'How well do you know Kusborski?' I asked.

'Kusborski?' She really didn't seem to know.

'Your compatriot, the cop,' I said.

'Oh, I didn't know his name,' she said. 'I don't know him at all, I've never seen him before or heard his name.' I nodded, that left a question that needed answering, but not by her.

'What are you looking for?' I asked instead.

'A gold medallion.'

'Just one?'

'Yes.'

'There seems to be a lot of fuss for just one gold medallion.'

'It seems that way to you because . . . well, let's say there's more to it than its own value.'

'I expect there is,' I said. 'Okay, tell me about the medallion.'

She delved into her handbag and handed something to me. I took it. It was round, about the size of a five-penny piece but about three times as thick. On one side was a deeply-embossed design resembling a rose. I turned it over and the back was smooth. It was made of gold. I looked at her inquiringly.

'The medallion we are looking for is like that on the face, but on the back, cut into the smooth side, is a five-figure number.'

'What number?' I said without thinking much about what I was saying.

She looked at me with an unfathomable expression in her eyes. 'If we knew that, Mr Morgan, we wouldn't need to find the real medallion.'

'Okay,' I said. 'So we're looking for a gold medallion about an inch across that might or might not be lying about on that site up at Cobham, and which you all seem to think Stanley might or might not have found without telling anyone.'

'Yes, that and anything we can find out about the identity of the man whose skeleton he found.'

'I would think that part of it will be easier than trying to find the medallion,' I said.

'Maybe.'

'I may be talking myself out of a job,' I said, 'but you don't need me to try to identify the skeleton. If anyone can, it isn't going to be a small-time private detective in England.'

'Who is it going to be?' she asked. Before I had time to answer I heard the sound of a vehicle coming up the drive. I glanced at my watch. It would be Stanley. I had lost track of the time. I felt a swell of panic in my chest as I remembered the last time Stanley found me alone in the company of a woman.

'Christ,' I muttered. 'Listen, this is Stanley. Don't say anything more than you have to. And agree with everything I say. And, most important, behave as if you don't like me.'

She smiled. 'What makes you think that will be difficult?' she said.

'For Christ's sake, it isn't a game,' I said, and something of my panic must have shown in my voice or in my face because she frowned and then nodded her head quickly as Stanley came into the room.

'Hello, Harry,' he said. 'Look what I found to . . .' His voice trailed off as he saw Selena Cantrell. He stood there looking at her, his smile dimmed but an odd light flickered in his eyes.

'This is my cousin, Stanley Meadows,' I said. 'Stanley this is a client of mine, her name is . . . Mrs Mason. Her husband is outside. Did you see him as you came in?'

He shook his head slowly and then I heard a noise outside and the lawyer reappeared. I sent up a small prayer of thanks to whoever it is up there that looks after private-inquiry agents in times of need.

'Ah, here he is now,' I said. I glanced urgently at Selena Cantrell. She stood up gracefully and walked over to Mason, slipped her arm through his and kissed him on the cheek. He looked astonished.

'Hello dear,' she said to him. 'Ready to go?' He nodded dumbly. 'Good-bye then, Mr Morgan, and good-bye, Mr Meadows.' She smiled at Stanley and turned to walk out. Mason had no alternative but to go with her. I followed them out and walked with them to the end of the drive, where Mason had brought the car.

'Come to the hotel tomorrow,' she said as she slid gracefully into the car. 'We can make a start and you can tell me why you think you're the wrong man for the job.' Mason started the car as she closed the door. Then she wound down her window and proved that she shared most women's natural curiosity. 'You can also tell me what all that was about.' She wound the window up again and the car went off down the road.

I walked back up to the house. Stanley was already watching television. He seemed to have taken my little performance at face value. I sat in a chair and let my thoughts ramble. I had been there for about ten minutes before I remembered Kusborski.

'I'm going down the road for a few minutes, Stanley,' I said. 'Then I'll come back and make your dinner.' He nodded. I remembered what he had started to say when he had first come in. 'You found something today, did you?'

He grinned hugely and bounded to his feet. 'Yes, Harry, look.' He reached down behind the settee and showed me the latest addition to his collection. I took it from him.

'It's very nice,' I said and handed it back. I didn't think a motor-cycle mudguard would do much to further the case of Tony Capelli.

As I reached the door he spoke to me. 'The lady was very pretty,' he said. I turned back to him and there was no guile in his eyes. My little piece of play-acting seemed to have worked.

'Yes,' I said. 'She is.'

I went down the road to the Cyder House, which seemed as good a place as any. I guessed right. Kusborski was sitting there nursing a large Scotch. He grinned as I came in.

'Well, did she hire you?'

'Yes.'

'To do what?'

'Find the identity of the skeleton.'

'That all?'

'She is also looking for a medallion.'

'Ah, so she told you that.'

'You know about it?'

'Yes. The Rose Medallion. Or rather one of them.'

'How many are there?' I asked, expecting the answer to run at least into thousands.

'Three,' he said. I felt curiously disappointed. 'At least we've made a couple of gains,' he added.

'Name them.'

'One, we have a foot in their camp, and the other is you're now getting paid for your involvement.'

I nodded and thought for a moment about the unwritten rules of confidentiality. I didn't say anything to Kusborski. I would save that for later when I had found the right way to ask him to answer something else that was bothering me.

'Do you want running back to town?' I asked.

'Haven't booked in anywhere yet,' he said. 'Remember, we talked of me staying with you so I could pay you out of my expenses. I nodded and I didn't bother to point out that we had already solved that particular problem. If he wanted to stay close to me then I might as well let him. At least until I knew a little more about him, and why he seemed to need me as much as he said he did. As we walked back up the road to the cottage it occurred to me that although, at last, people had started telling me things, with every piece of information I had been given I seemed to get at least two more questions that needed answering. It didn't seem to be the right balance.

CHAPTER NINE

Stanley didn't seem to mind our temporary lodger; indeed the way Kusborski had talked to him on the earlier occasion had left a favourable impression with both of us. When Stanley discovered that Kusborski was a New York cop he reacted as any small boy might have done, any small boy whose favourite form of entertainment was television. I sat and watched Stanley's face as Kusborski talked. The delight and pleasure that were there should have made me feel happy but they didn't. I saw instead the massive frame, almost seven feet tall, the bulging muscles and the incredible strength that lay in his huge hands. It depressed me again.

The following morning I dropped Kusborski in town; he said he wanted to talk to Peters at the police station, and I gave him a key to my office and arranged to meet him there later in the day. Selena Cantrell was waiting for me at the hotel.

'Have you had breakfast?' she asked. I told her that breakfast was something I usually managed to do without. She suggested that we sit in the gardens, as the day was already beginning to warm up. We sat in cane chairs by the pool and she took a pair of sunglasses from her bag and put them on. Whether she really needed them or whether she wanted to conceal her eyes from me, I didn't know. It didn't bother me very much one way or the other. People's eyes help when you are trying to tell if they are speaking the truth, but their hands give as much away. Sometimes more.

'Tell me about Kusborski,' she began.

'What is there to tell?' I said. 'He's a detective, a sergeant in the NYPD, and he's been sent here because we found the body of a former New York gangster.'

'Is that all?' she asked. I couldn't see why I was supposed to tell her Kusborski knew about the medallion.

'Yes,' I said.

She nodded her head slowly and I watched her hands. They lay loosely clasped in her lap, no twisting, no twitching.

'Do you believe him?' Her question was unexpected and I thought carefully about it before I answered.

'I can't think of any reason why I shouldn't,' I said. As I spoke I could think of at least two reasons why I shouldn't. I wondered if my eyes were concealing my thoughts. My hands certainly were; they were in my pockets.

'Very well. You said yesterday you were not the man to find the real identity of the skeleton.'

'That's right.'

'Who is the man then?'

'I didn't have a particular person in mind,' I said. 'There are ways, ways that are more readily available to other people. For example, an inquiry agent in New York could do it better than I could.'

'No,' she said emphatically. 'Not New York. Can you do it from here?'

'I expect so.'

'Tell me,' she said musingly. 'If a New York private detective could do it, then presumably a New York policeman could do it at least as easily.' I nodded; she had asked one of the questions I had been asking myself.

'Maybe,' I said.

'Are you planning on telling Kusborski what you find out? Are you planning on telling him what you and I talk about?'

she asked. I shook my head. 'Have you told him anything so far?' I thought about the conversation we had had the previous evening. I had told him about the medallion but he had already known of its existence.

'No,' I lied. Her hands moved in her lap and I wondered if she believed me. 'Tell me,' I asked, 'does the medallion have a name?'

'Yes, they . . . it is called the Rose Medallion.'

'They?' I asked gently.

She bit her lip in annoyance. 'There were three,' she said. I nodded slightly. 'You knew?' she asked.

'Something Kusborski said,' I replied. That seemed to satisfy her, and it seemed also to satisfy her that I wasn't playing a double game. I wasn't; as far as I could see it was already much more complicated than that.

'What do you plan to do?' she asked.

'About the skeleton, I'll make a telephone call when I get back to the office,' I said. 'The questions I'll ask may take some time to answer, so while I'm waiting I'll make a start on looking for the medallion.'

'At the site?'

'No. Needles in haystacks have nothing on looking for that. No, I have a friend who has one of those little metal detectors. I'll get him out there looking for it. It may be that the medallion has already been found, so I'll make inquiries among local coin dealers and jewellers.'

She seemed disappointed. 'Is that all?'

'It will do for now. This is what I want you and Mason to do.' I outlined what I had in mind for them and she agreed. She was puzzled but she didn't ask for an explanation, which suited me because I couldn't have given her one. When I finished she nodded. As I rose to leave she stopped me, placing her hand on mine. It felt cool and pleasant.

'What was that all about – yesterday, when Stanley came in?'

'I'll tell you when I know you better.'

'If you ever do,' she said.

'If I ever do.'

I left her sitting in the sun and went out to the car. I drove a short distance to a telephone box and from which I could see the hotel. I rang my second-hand car dealer friend and asked him if he knew where I could lay my hands on a metal detector. He told me his son had one and I arranged to borrow it from him, for a small charge – people never do things for nothing anymore. Then I rang Tommy Andrews at the site and told him what I wanted, and he agreed to pick up the metal detector and start searching the site. Then I phoned my office to see if Kusborski was there. He wasn't. I thought about trying to reach him at the police station, but it was unlikely that I would endear myself to Peters if he knew I was working closely with his transatlantic colleague. I came out of the telephone box and sat waiting in the car. After about ten minutes I tried again, and he was there. I told him which drawer I kept the telephone directories in, and he agreed to spend a couple of hours running up my telephone bill while he rang round various coin dealers and jewellers. As I finished the call, I saw Selena Cantrell and Mason drive out of the hotel and turn towards Leatherhead. I followed, well back, because I knew where they were going.

We were through Leatherhead and on the A24 going up towards London before I was sure I had spotted the Granada. It was behind me, and had been lying so far back I hadn't noticed it at first. I dropped out of the chase by turning into a side road. I reversed into someone's driveway and waited. The Granada went past the road end, and, as far as I could see, neither of the men in the front seats looked my way. I pulled out of the driveway just as the owner of the house came out of the front door, looking all bristly and full of fight. Some people get very territorial about a little piece of gravel drive.

Just before we all turned off into Streatham I stopped at a telephone box and rang the inquiry agent Miss Cantrell was going to. I told him what I wanted and he agreed. Even he wouldn't do it for nothing. He wanted a favour of me. I told him I'd ring him from the office when I got back. I hung around near the telephone box and waited. They must have had difficulty in parking – Streatham isn't the best place in the world for that – it was almost an hour before they reappeared. I joined my place in the caravan behind the Granada and we all went back towards East Horsley. Once we were past Leatherhead I closed up on the Granada. Tommy had been insistent on how abruptly they had disappeared the night he had tailed them.

As it was, it proved easy. They trailed the first car back to Thatchers and one of the men—he was very tall and thin and I assumed it was Martinelli—climbed out and drifted into the hotel. The other man drove the Granada out again and went back the way we had come. When he turned off the road, I was less than a hundred yards behind him and I marked the spot carefully. When I drove past, it was one of those entrances into a private road that leads to more than one house. There were three signposts just off the main road. That meant I had tied the opposition down to one of three houses. That was near enough for me. I made a mental note of the names of the houses and went back to Guildford.

In the office Kusborski was making like an efficient detective, New York style. He had his feet on my desk, my bottle of whisky and a glass in front of him, and the telephone cradled under his chin. From the way he shook his head as I came in, I guessed he hadn't got anywhere. I pulled up the other chair and poured myself a small drink. When he finished the call he was making he crossed out another name in the telephone book and looked at me.

'No luck?' I asked.

'No. Nothing. I've a few more before I give up. What

have you been doing?' I couldn't see why I shouldn't tell him; after all I was going to need his help.

'I've been finding out where Alda and Martinelli are staying,' I said.

His eyes lit up. 'Where? How did you find them?' he asked. I told him, grinning.

'I sent Miss Cantrell and Mr Mason on a wild-goose chase. Our other friends tailed them, as I hoped they might. I followed them.'

He grinned back at me. 'Neat,' he said. He seemed very pleased, and I was pleased that he was pleased. I almost wished I trusted him.

It didn't take much effort to find out which of the three houses Alda and Martinelli were at. I rang an estate agent friend and gave him the names of the houses. He rang me back in about ten minutes.

'Tree Cottage is the only one that is rented,' he told me. 'The other two are owner-occupied.'

'Did you get a name for the tenant?' I asked.

'Merrit, Alexander Merrit and he speaks with an American accent.'

'Thanks,' I said and waited.

'That's a pint you owe me,' he said, just to prove my point. I hung up and thought about calling the man in Streatham. I decided not to bother. If he really wanted a favour he would ring me soon enough, and after Kusborski's efforts my telephone bill would be unpleasantly large already.

'Tree Cottage,' I told Kusborski. 'Rented in the name of Merrit. Mean anything?'

'No. Could mean there are more than just two of them. Any ideas?' he asked.

'I thought we might poke around and see what they want?'

'They want what we all want,' he said.

'Probably. At least it wouldn't do any harm to know if they know more or less than we do.'

'Less, probably. Otherwise why would they be following Mason and the Cantrell woman?'

'Yes,' I said. 'You're probably right.' I reached for the telephone again and called the estate agent.

'Make it two pints,' I said.

'What do you want to know?'

'Is there a burglar alarm?'

'Are you up to something, Harry?' he asked.

'No. I have a client who might want to rent when the present tenants move out, and he's fussy.'

'Okay,' he said and rang off. He rang me back within minutes.

'No burglar alarm, but if he wants it for a long stay something can be done.'

'Great,' I said and hung up.

Kusborski looked at me. 'Tonight?' he asked.

'Might as well. Unless you have anything else planned.'

'No, but that leaves the rest of the day,' he said.

I pointed at the telephone book. 'Let your fingers do the walking,' I told him and went out. I drove the Volvo down to Bramley. I rarely called on Julie unannounced, but I hadn't felt like calling her in front of Kusborski, and highly personal calls from telephone boxes always seem unsatisfactory. I rang the bell on the front door and waited. I thought I had wasted my time, and then I heard her coming down the stairs. She opened the door.

'What do you want?' she said and her tone was anything but friendly.

'To see you,' I said. She hesitated and then stepped back and I went in. She led the way into the sitting-room and I suddenly realised that in all the time I had been going there, I'd never been in that room before. Just the bedroom at the back of the house, the bathroom and the kitchen when it was my turn to make the coffee. The room had a curiously un-Julie-like look about it. Everything neat and precise and with absolutely no character at all. Quite impersonal. I sat on the settee and she stood looking at me. She looked edgy.

'Is everything okay?' I asked.

'Why shouldn't it be?' she said defensively.

'No reason,' I backpedalled. I knew I had done the wrong thing in turning up unannounced, but it shouldn't have thrown her that way. I heard a floorboard creak upstairs. I looked up. 'Are the kids home?' I asked, and as I did so everything registered. 'Who is he?' I asked. She made a gesture, half embarrassment, half defiance.

'You don't own me, Harry,' she said. I stood up and went to her. I wanted to touch her but I knew that to do so would be wrong at that moment.

'Christ, Julie,' I said softly. 'I never thought I did. You have a life and so do I.'

'Just ships that pass?' she said, and the note of bitterness in her voice shocked me.

'You know it was more than that,' I said, and even then I noticed cold-bloodedly how easily I had dropped into the past tense. She nodded her head jerkily.

'Yes, I'm sorry, Harry. Don't think badly of me. It's just that, well, I want something more than you were prepared to give me.' I looked at her and she looked up into my eyes. Tears were already forming in hers.

'What?' I asked.

She shook her head and the action made the first tear begin to roll down her cheek. 'You have to ask, haven't you? You would never have thought of it on your own.'

'What, for Christ's sake?' I said.

'A home,' she waved her hand at the room, 'not like this. A real home for me and the kids.'

'You mean ...' I stopped, gestured up at the ceiling. 'Does he want to marry you?' I asked.

'I think so,' she said.

I nodded my head. 'I never thought that way,' I said.

'I knew you didn't, Harry.'

'I'm sorry,' I said. She nodded and moved closer to me. It seemed right to touch her then. I put my arms around her.

'What's his name?' I asked.

'Paul Jackson. He's a rep with a catering firm. I met him when he called at one of the hotels I was working at.'

'I'd better go,' I said. I kissed her on the top of her head. Her hair smelled faintly of cooking. I had never thought of her in a domestic way before and then, when it seemed the right way to think of her, it was also too late. I let myself out and got into the Volvo. Just along the road was a Viva estate car I hadn't noticed when I went in. I guessed it was his car. The detective in me recorded the registration number as I drove away.

I went back to the cottage and spent the rest of the afternoon lying on the bed staring at the ceiling. I was neither happier nor wiser when it was time to go to the office and collect Kusborski.

CHAPTER TEN

Tree Cottage was a large rambling house, probably built in the mid-thirties after the rash of poor-quality housing had dried up, and before building was almost halted by the war. Money had not been spared and the result of unlimited funds and a team of craftsmen, unaware that they were a dying breed, had produced a neo-Georgian residence designed with almost unbelievably bad taste. Its present-day value would have been approximately equivalent to eighty years' wages for one of the men who had built it. I thought there might be a moral there somewhere. It was the farthest from the main road of the three houses that shared the private road. Kusborski and I had padded down to it, the big man moving softly and easily in the darkness. We had made plans before we set out, and with Kusborski driving we had left the car a hundred yards down the road.

When we came to the edge of the lawn that surrounded the house we split up, Kusborski moving off to the left, me to the right. When we met up at the far side of the house, neither of us had seen anything and we moved closer to the house before stopping for a hurried, whispered conference. There were lights in two rooms, one on the ground floor overlooking the lawn at the rear of the house, and one upstairs at the front. Kusborski suggested that I take the upstairs room but I backed out of that, not that I have no head for heights, but I had seen from the way he moved that he was less likely to make a noise in getting up to a first-floor window. He agreed and we separated.

The window of the ground-floor room was a square-fronted bay, the glass arranged in diamond-shaped leaded lights, and inside the room hung heavy, patterned curtains. At first I thought I wouldn't be able to see inside, but then I noticed that at the top of the window the curtains were not completely closed, and with something to stand on I would be able to see into the room. I went in search of the something I needed to give me that extra few inches. At the bottom of the lawn was a heavy timber slab table with four chairs arranged around it. The chairs were no light-weights, and by the time I had lugged one to the window I was sweating and beginning to think it hadn't been such a good idea after all. I positioned the chair carefully outside the window and climbed up, balancing myself with one hand against the window-frame. I peered in through the gap in the curtains. There were two men in the room: Alda and Martinelli. I stayed where I was for a moment and then I felt the chair moving slightly. I climbed down again and repositioned it. As I was doing that, I heard the sound of a door opening inside the room and voices rumbling quietly. I climbed back up again and looked in through the window. A third man had joined the other two. He was seated in a chair with his back to the window, and I could see only the back of his head. Martinelli was talking to him but the words were indistinct. One of the top small windows was open to let in air and I decided to move around to that. Even if I couldn't see in through it, I should at least be able to hear what was being said. I clambered down again and moved the chair. When I had it in the right place I straightened, ready to climb up again.

I heard a soft rushing sound in the air, almost as if a bird was flying near. I started to turn my head, and as I did so I registered that someone was standing behind me, and the soft rushing sound wasn't a bird. It was the automatic intake of breath a man makes as he prepares to expend energy. The energy that particular man planned to expend was directed into a blow that landed on the back of my head just behind the left ear. A large black hole opened up in the ground and I tried to jump into it. Something seemed to stop me and I was vaguely aware of sounds, and I felt a curious floating motion of my body that wasn't entirely unpleasant. Then the floating motion stopped and I heard a bell start to ring, and then I heard the rushing intake of breath again and the black hole opened even wider. I tried to jump into it again and this time nothing stopped me.

I heard a voice that I recognised and I thought that perhaps I was just having a nightmare. I tried opening my eyes and there were faces looking at me. I recognised one of them and knew that it was a nightmare. I closed my eyes and opened them again. The face was still there. I sat up and pain jolted through me from the back of my head. I reached up and touched the place. There was a lump that hadn't been there when I had started out, and it hurt like hell. I struggled to my feet and no one offered to help me. I looked at the faces all around me. There were four. Two of the faces had uniforms below and dark caps with silver-coloured badges above. I didn't have to be told they were the constabulary – after all I am a detective. The third face I didn't recognise; it had fluffy white hair above it and a dressing-gown below. It also had an expression of acute indignation on it. The fourth face belonged in my nightmare. I smiled at it and it sneered back at me. It looked as if Sergeant Fowler's prayers had been answered.

'What happened?' I asked, fully aware that it wasn't the most original thing I could have said.

'Christ, Morgan, I've been waiting for this,' Fowler said. 'This time the book gets thrown at you.'

'For what?' I asked.

'For what? For enough to put you out of business for ever.' He paused. 'You've had it, Morgan.' I began to feel dizzy and slightly sick. The pain at the back of my head was worse.

'Have you called an ambulance?' I asked.

'What for?' he asked.

'For me, you silly bastard,' I told him, and I felt my legs start to go. I slid down to the ground again.

I knew that I was in hospital before I opened my eyes. The smell and the sounds couldn't have been produced anywhere else. I opened my eyes and looked around. The room was small; apparently I rated a room to myself. There was a man in a white coat who looked like a doctor, a policeman in uniform, and Inspector Peters. Fowler wasn't there. I looked at the man I took to be the doctor.

'Will I live?' I asked him. He grinned amiably.

'I expect so,' he said. He had a Scottish accent. 'We haven't found any evidence of fracture and there are no signs of concussion – yet.' He nodded at Peters and walked out of the room. Peters came over to the bedside and sat on the edge of the one chair that stood there.

'Before you start,' I said, 'what time is it?'

'Five o'clock. In the morning,' he told me.

I thought rapidly. I hadn't bothered to put the troops in to look after Stanley, because as far as I knew the only people likely to cause him any harm were Alda and Martinelli, and as I had planned to be watching them there hadn't seemed to be any need. 'You don't owe me any favours,' I said. He nodded in agreement. 'But can someone have a look to see if Stanley is okay?' I asked. He thought about it for a moment. 'Not Fowler,' I added. He stood up and walked over to the uniformed man who was standing by the door. Peters spoke to him for a few moments and the man left the room. Peters came back and sat on the chair again. This time he sat on it properly and looked almost relaxed.

'Why don't you and Fowler get on?' he asked.

'For the same reason you and he don't, I expect,' was my answer. He smiled and there was none of the hesitancy that he usually showed. It had been an act after all.

'He wanted to throw the book at you,' he said.

'So I gathered. What stopped him?'

'I did.'

'Why?'

'Very little of it would have stuck, and anything that did would probably have been unjustified.'

'What . . .?' I started to speak, but he interrupted.

'I think I should ask a few questions,' he said quietly. That seemed reasonable, and there was always the chance that from his questions I would be able to find a few answers for myself. 'First of all, what were you doing at Bennett's End?' I stared at him for a moment trying to work out what he was talking about. Then the name registered. It was one of the other houses in the private road. The one nearest the main road. That accounted for the floating feeling. I had been carried from Tree Cottage and dumped outside another house and then, presumably, hit again. I thought fast and tried to ignore the headache that was beginning to make its presence felt.

'I was passing the road end,' I improvised. 'I saw someone moving about and he looked suspicious. I stopped the car, went back to investigate, and someone hit me from behind. That's all I remember.' He looked at me from beneath hooded eyelids. I could tell that he didn't believe me. Hardly anyone would have believed a story as patently weak as that one. Surprisingly he nodded his head.

'You could be telling me the truth I suppose,' he said.

'I am,' I said.

'But then again you could be telling me the lies that Fowler thinks you're capable of.'

'Fowler is . . .' Peters held up a hand.

'Sergeant Fowler is a police officer with an excellent record, and a pronounced sense of what is right and what is wrong. He thinks you are wrong. He thinks you were at the house to commit an offence.'

'What do *you* think?' I asked, trying to make it sound as if that was more important than what Fowler thought. Which it was.

'I think you were following someone in the line of an inquiry and you got unlucky.' He was close enough, but not so close that I couldn't afford to let him have a little encouragement.

'Yes,' I said. 'I must be losing my grip.'

'It could happen to us all,' he said. We looked at one another for a moment. He put his hands on the edge of the bed and leaned forward. 'Has your inquiry anything, anything at all, to do with the skeleton your cousin found?'

'No,' I said firmly.

'And nothing to do with whatever it was Kusborski came over here to look for?' I shook my head. He sat back and thought for a moment. 'I don't think there is anything more for the moment, Mr Morgan,' he said, 'I'm not closing this matter. Not yet. I hope that you will not give me cause to follow up some of Sergeant Fowler's suggestions.' I hoped I wouldn't as well. He walked over to the door.

'Can I go home?' I asked. He turned round.

'You can for me,' he said. 'It's up to the medical people; that was a very heavy blow you sustained.' He turned away and went out before he could be accused of expressing concern for my welfare. I looked at the door, and after a moment, it reopened and the Scots doctor came in.

'How are you feeling?' he asked.

I thought about it. 'Apart from the headache I feel okay. Can I leave?' He pursed his lips and looked at me.

'I can't stop you.'

'All right, I'll rephrase the question. Would you advise me to leave?'

'No.'

'What is the worst that could happen?' I asked.

'Concussion doesn't always appear immediately. The blows could have been worse than they seem. And they were bad enough to begin with.' He seemed to be confirming my thoughts that I had been hit twice.

'Any idea what I was hit with?'

'I told the police it looked like a very heavy object covered in something soft. The skin wasn't broken. You were hit twice. Almost in the same place but not quite. Whoever did it had done it before.' It was almost as if the doctor was commenting on the surgical skill of a colleague. I reached a decision.

'I'll leave,' I said. 'Can I have my clothes please?'

He shrugged his shoulders. Clearly if I wanted to be an idiot he wasn't going to lose any sleep over it.

By the time I had dressed and fought my way through the small jungle of red-tape that preceded my departure into the wide world it was almost eight o'clock. I called for a taxi and let it take me to Shackleford. Peters had organised a watch on the house and there was a police car at the foot of the drive. The two uniformed men in it were having a quiet cigarette.

'Everything okay?' I asked.

'Yes,' the one in the driving seat told me. 'He's just gone off in a blue Transit van. We were told to keep a watch on him here. Not to follow.'

'Thanks,' I said and let the taxi take me up to the door. I wandered around and saw that Stanley hadn't bothered to make his bed or prepare himself any breakfast. There was a funny smell in the air and I traced it to the kettle. He had forgotten to put any water in it before trying to make himself some tea. I thought about having a tidy round and then thought better of it. I told the taxi-driver to take me to the office. Kusborski was there. I sat in the chair opposite the desk and found that from there I could see the damp patch. I stood up and told him to get out of my chair. I flopped down in the seat; it was the more comfortable of the two. I wondered if whisky would help and came to the conclusion that it probably wouldn't. I looked at Kusborski, who hadn't spoken.

'All right,' I said. 'Explain.'

'I hoped you might be doing that,' he said.

'Why?'

'I found a ladder in the garage,' he said. 'I went up it to look in the upstairs room that was showing a light. I couldn't see anything or hear anyone moving about, so I decided to try and get into the house. I opened a window and then came for you before I went in. When I reached the ground-floor window with the light in it, you were missing. There was a chair in the middle of the flower-bed. I started to look around for you and then I heard a commotion down the road. I backtracked and there you were, laid out in the middle of the lawn of the house nearest to the road, with a burglar alarm ringing and a white-haired old guy in a dressing-gown jumping around getting hysterical. Then I heard a car coming and I figured it must be the police, so I decided to move on. I took the car and came back here.'

'A burglar alarm was ringing?'

'Yes. At the house, what was it called – Bennett something?'

'Bennett's End,' I filled in for him.

'Yes. The alarm was ringing,' he repeated. I thought about that for a moment.

'I wonder why,' I said.

'Don't you know?'

'No.'

'What did happen?' he asked.

'Someone hit me.'

'I guessed that.'

'That's all.'

'What do you mean all.'

'Well,' I said, 'there was another guy in the house with Alda and Martinelli.'

'Did you recognise him?'

'No, I didn't see his face.'

'And then you were knocked out?'

'Yes, and I came to on the lawn of the other house and the place was full of policemen. Well there were three of them including my friend Sergeant Fowler.'

'What did you tell him?' He sounded concerned.

'Nothing. I didn't have anything *to* tell him. Anyway I passed out and woke up in hospital with Inspector Peters looking all worried and motherly.'

'What did you tell him?'

'The same as I told Fowler.' I thought for a moment. 'They don't know you're here, do they?'

He thought about telling me a lie and came to the conclusion that it would be a waste of time. 'No they don't. How did you guess?'

'Nothing specific. Things they said, things you said earlier all dropped into place. Why are you here?' I asked. 'And don't tell me the NYPD are playing spies without the knowledge of the English police, because I won't believe you.' He grinned and looked round the room.

'Is there any Scotch left?' he asked.

'Buy your own bloody whisky,' I growled at him. He grinned to show he hadn't taken offence, but I wasn't sure that none had been intended.

'Okay, Harry. I haven't been fair. You're right, of course,

I'm here on my own as a private citizen. Not that first time, of course. Then I came officially and, as you know, Peters knew I was here.'

'So what happened?'

'When you called me in New York and I found out who was sniffing around over here, I wanted to come back and find out what was going on. I asked my chief to let me and he said no. I had some leave coming so I took it, and here I am.'

'If your chief isn't interested, why are you?'

'Two reasons. One, well, let's call it old scores to settle.'

'And the other?'

'I want to hang something on the Capelli brothers. Either of them or preferably both of them.' It sounded reasonable. Just the kind of thing a big, honest policeman with a fine sense of duty would have said. I wanted to believe it.

'Is that all?' I asked.

'Yes,' he said simply. He paused. 'That's God's truth Harry.' He shouldn't have added that. I had almost decided to believe him.

'Okay,' I said. He sat there looking big and honest and a friend for life. I noticed he had a plaster on the back of his right hand. I didn't remember seeing it there before. But then observation hadn't been my strong suit all along.

'Let's have a drink,' he said.

'Not with my head,' I replied.

'Why not?' he asked, and I couldn't think of a good answer.

'Okay, but you're buying.'

'Of course,' he said. We went down the stairs, the big American detective and the not so big English one. I still couldn't understand what I was doing in the case. It must have been a hitherto hidden sense of public duty. Or something like that.

CHAPTER ELEVEN

It was a busy morning for telephone calls. I had five of them in quick succession and none of them brought good news. The first was from my estate-agent friend who told me that Tree Cottage was back on the market as the present tenant had left unexpectedly. I told him I would phone my client, then ring him back. I thought about that for a moment, and told Kusborski it would be an opportunity to have a look round. He agreed. I rang the estate agent back and told him I was sending someone down who wanted to look over the property. I gave Kusborski the address of the agent and we went off quietly down the stairs. The second call was from Michael Silver who said the old lady in Devon had responded to his letter by getting her solicitor to write to him. Did I still want to go on with it? I didn't, but I have a stubborn streak that pays little heed to reality. I said I did. The third call was from Selena Cantrell who told me that her legal-eagle friend John Mason hadn't shown up for breakfast and his bed hadn't been slept in. She said she was worried, and she sounded it. That surprised me, I'd had her marked down as harder than that. I told her I would be down there in a couple of hours but to ring me back if he showed up in the meantime. I tried to place a call to a friend of mine in the War Office but he wasn't there – in conference, his secretary told me; playing golf, my mind said. The fourth call was from Rosemary who said she had thought I would have rung her. I told her I had been left with the distinct impression that I was out of favour. She said she hadn't meant to convey that, and could she see me. I told her I had been in a slight accident and would ring her in a couple of days or so. She clucked and fussed like a mother hen, and I had to convince her that I wasn't at death's door. I had stood up to leave when the fifth call came in. It was Tommy.

'Find anything?' I asked.

'No. Unless you count three half-crowns, fourteen empty food cans and an assortment of scrap metal. That isn't why I called.'

'What's happened?'

'Nothing really but ... well, you know how particular Stanley is with keeping vehicles clean?'

'Yes.'

'Well, the big digger he's using to shift muck, you know, the one he was driving when he found the, er ...'

'Mr Bones,' I said.

'What? Oh, yes, joke. Yes the one he was using then.'

'What about it?'

'Last night he parked it as usual and cleaned the thick of the muck off it with a shovel as he always does. Not like the other buggers. They leave half a yard of mud on every night. Spreads all over the ...'

I felt we were getting off the subject. 'Tommy, what are you driving at?'

'What? Oh, sorry. Well, this morning it was covered in mud and Stanley got a bit upset, said someone had been using his machine ... Well I convinced him he was mistaken and he calmed down and went off quite happily.'

'Well, so what?' I asked.

'Well I started thinking,' Tommy replied. 'He *is* particular about keeping machines clean and, well, in view of what's been happening around here, I wondered if someone had been using it during the night.'

I thought for a moment. 'Okay, Tommy. I'll come out. I have to call at East Horsley first.'

'At the hotel?'

'Yes.'

'When are you going to tell me what it's all about?'

'I told you, I'd tell you when I know myself.'

'You mean you still don't know?'

'No.'

'And I thought you were a detective.'

'So did I,' I said.

I drove down to the hotel and found Selena Cantrell by the pool again. No sunglasses, although the sun was just as strong. Maybe she didn't have anything to hide this time.

'He hasn't been seen since after dinner last night,' she told me.

'You dined together?'

'Yes.'

'Then what?'

'He said he didn't feel well and went up to his room.'

'What did you do?' I asked.

She looked at me as if about to tell me to mind my own business, and then seemed to accept that the question was asked in the line of duty.

'I went to my room,' she said. 'I had some telephone calls to make.' I looked at her inquiringly but she clearly drew the line at telling me who the calls were to.

'Then what?'

'Then I went to bed.'

'What time was that?'

'We finished dinner about nine, and I spoke on the telephone for over an hour. It would be about ten-thirty. Maybe a little before.'

'You didn't leave your room?'

'No.'

'And you didn't go to Mason's room?'

She looked angrily at me. 'No, why should I?'

'He was ill,' I said calmly. 'It would have been a natural thing to do.'

'No I didn't.' She seemed slightly mollified.

'And you didn't call him on the telephone?'

'No. We ...' she hesitated. 'We had been arguing at dinner. I was angry with him.'

'I'm not prying,' I said, to conceal the fact that I was. 'Could the argument you had be a reason for him going off without telling you?'

'No,' she answered quickly.

'Okay,' I said. 'I'll start looking but I won't pretend it will be easy. I haven't a clue where to begin.' I stood up to leave.

'You said you would make a start on tracing the identity of the skeleton. Have you?'

'No I haven't,' I admitted. 'The man I want was missing when I rang him this morning. I'll get on to him later.' She nodded and then as I turned to go she caught her breath.

'What happened to you?' she said. I turned and realised she had seen the bruising that was visible under my hair.

'Problems,' I said.

'Connected with this?' she asked.

'This, you mean Mason?'

She shook her head. 'No, I mean with the case, any of it?'

'Yes,' I said. 'I expect it was.'

'Who did it?' she asked.

'I don't know,' I said, which was very nearly true.

When I arrived at the site, Tommy was in his office, speaking on the telephone in a subdued bellow to some poor soul at the other end who appeared to have earned Tommy's wrath by failing to deliver to the site a few thousand cubic feet of hardcore at the time he had promised. I waited until he had finished.

'Bastards,' he said. 'They think they've got me over a barrel and they're trying it on.'

'Have they?' I asked.

'Have they what?'

'Got you over a barrel?'

'Of course they have but I'm convincing them the reverse is the case.' He grinned widely. He enjoyed his work. It would have given a lesser man an ulcer the size of a fried egg but Tommy thrived on adversity.

'I'm here,' I told him.

'Yes. I might be wasting your time but . . .'

' . . . then again you might not,' I finished for him. He nodded and stood up.

'Come on,' he said. We went out of the office and climbed into a Land-Rover and went lurching off down the track that followed the excavation for the foundation of the motorway. He drove erratically, and I was grateful we were not on a road. Perhaps he would have driven with more care if we had been. After we had gone about five hundred yards from the office he pulled over and stopped. He pointed to where four large yellow machines were scraping away at the earth.

'That one is Stanley,' he said. They all looked alike to me. He gestured away to his left. 'As far as I can tell all the newly-turned earth is from here to where they're working now. In this weather earth dries out pretty quickly and you get a pronounced colour change. If someone has been using Stanley's bucket, then it must have been from here on.'

I climbed down from the Land-Rover and walked over to the pile of earth. It rose to about three feet over my head and was about eight feet wide at the base. It stretched away to where the diggers were working, a distance of about two hundred yards. I turned back to Tommy.

'It couldn't be anywhere else on the site where earth has been moved?'

'No.'

'Certain?'

'Positive,' he said. I took his word for it. As far as I could see, earth was earth, but it was his business – he should know what he was talking about.

'And you're sure the digger was used last night?' I asked.

'I'm not, but Stanley is. Do you want to ask him yourself?' I looked to where Stanley's machine was beavering away.

'No,' I said. I thought for a moment. Something rather unpleasant floated into my mind. 'What happens to this pile of earth?' I asked Tommy.

'Later it will be landscaped. Make the view pretty for the passing motorist.'

'How will it be landscaped?'

'How? With a scraper. The muck'll be shifted about until it's level enough to grow grass on and then it will be seeded and nature will do the rest.'

'So this mound of earth will be disturbed again.'

'Yes.'

'What about this?' I pointed down at the ground I stood on, the hundred-feet-wide slash that had been carved through the countryside.

'This gets covered in hardcore, and then cement and reinforcing, and then more cement, and finally an asphalt covering.' The unpleasant thought grew stronger.

'Can you tell if someone has dug deeper anywhere here and then filled it in again?'

'I expect so. What are you thinking about?'

'Someone hiding something, not looking for something,' I told him.

'What?'

'I've no idea,' I said, and wished it was true.

'Let's have a look,' he said. We walked across the hundred-feet scar and then back again about two paces farther on. Tommy's head was bent as if in prayer. He reminded me of the movies I'd seen as a small boy, where the old Indian Scout could tell if anyone had passed that way by looking for bent blades of grass. There wasn't any grass for Tommy, but as it turned out he was as good as any old Indian Scout would have been. I had given up; I couldn't see anything but earth anyway, and I was sitting in the Land-Rover when he called me. When I reached him he pointed down at the ground.

'Someone has been working here,' he said. I looked down. I couldn't see anything exceptional. 'See, the blade marks go the wrong way.' Tommy went on. 'They should finish by scraping in that direction. Just here the marks go the other way.' He was right; they did. 'Well?'

'I suppose we'd better open it up,' I said.

'I'll get Stanley,' he said.

'No.' I must have shouted because he looked at me in surprise.

'Okay. I'll get one of the other guys. Harry, what do you think is down there?' I shook my head.

'This isn't the time for guesses, Tommy. Get the man with the machine.' He drove off towards the four machines and moments later he was on his way back with one of the yellow monsters lumbering behind.

Tommy marked off the area he wanted the man to uncover. It took time because it was buried deep. It was wrapped in a thick, opaque plastic sheet. It could have been something other than a body but I didn't think it was. I kicked away the muck that covered it and started to unroll the sheet.

'Shouldn't we wait for the police to do that?' Tommy asked.

'Yes,' I said. 'We should.' I carried on unrolling the sheet. When the body was in view it was laid face downwards and the back of his head looked vaguely familiar. In the middle of the back of his jacket was a small neat hole. I rolled him over. The hole on the other side was neither small nor neat. Behind me I heard the digger driver and Tommy being sick. I looked at the craggy face. I told the driver to stay where he was and keep everyone away, particularly Stanley. Then I climbed into the driving seat of the Land-Rover and told Tommy to get in. It was time to get Inspector Peters. And after that I would have to ring Selena Cantrell and tell her that I was a clever detective. Without even trying I had found her missing friend. George Capelli would have to find a new lawyer. John Mason had hung up his shingle for the last time.

CHAPTER TWELVE

Inspector Peters was decidedly unhappy. And he said so in language that I found slightly shocking, but only because I kept thinking of him as resembling the vicar I had known. Sergeant Fowler, on the other hand, looked positively radiant. His sneer was absent for once and there was a smile of true pleasure on his face. This time he was sure he had me. We were sitting in Tommy's office. Peters and Fowler had looked at and then left the body to the attentions of the forensic boys. I had managed to get Stanley sent away before the law arrived, and all I really wanted to do was go somewhere and lie down. My head hurt.

'Tell me your story again, Morgan,' Peters said, and I didn't miss the fact that he had dropped the Mister. I was off his list of favourite people. So I told him my story again. I didn't miss very much out, apart from Kusborski, and the fact that I knew who Mason was, and the fact that I had telephoned Selena Cantrell to tell her about the murder. After all, Peters didn't know who she was, although he would very probably catch up with her fast. Unless she took advantage of my warning and caught the next plane across the Atlantic. He listened in silence. I could tell he didn't believe he had heard the full story. Unfortunately there wasn't anything he could do to unravel things, not right then. So after another hour of it he gave up and told me I could go.

'Thanks,' I said lightly. 'I'll be seeing you.'

'You will, Morgan,' he said. 'You will.'

I drove down the road towards Guildford and watched my rear-view mirror carefully until I spotted Fowler's Marina. I stopped at the first telephone box I came to and rang my office. Kusborski was there.

'Get lost,' I told him. 'Don't go to the cottage and don't come to the office again.'

'How will I reach you?' he asked.

I thought for a moment. 'Telephone me at the pub tonight. The Cyder House. And wherever you go don't use your real name.' I hung up and climbed back into the car and went to the office. I sat at the desk and awaited for inspiration to strike. It didn't. Later I rang the War Office and my friend was in. I told him what I wanted to know, and he said he doubted very much if it was possible to get that information.

'It's important,' I told him.

'How important?' he asked.

'Matter of life and death important,' I said.

'Whose life and death?' he asked.

'Mine,' I told him. He seemed impressed and told me he would do what he could.

The rest of the day dragged by so slowly I thought it must be a side effect of the bump on the back of my head. About four o'clock the telephone rang. A rapid pip-pip disappeared as my caller pushed the right coin into the right slot. It was Selena Cantrell.

'Where are you?' I asked.

'Is it safe?' she asked.

'The telephone won't be tapped,' I said hopefully.

'I'm at Heathrow. My flight leaves in about thirty minutes.'

'Good girl,' I said.

'Have you found out anything?'

'No.'

'I'll call you from New York tomorrow,' she said.

'Make it the ...' I was interrupted by more pips so I waited until she had pushed in more coins. 'I'll call you, the day after tomorrow,' I said. 'Have a sheet of paper and a pen ready. I might have some questions to ask. Some inquiries I might want making over there.'

'I'll do what I can,' she said.

'Whatever you can't do, I'm sure your friend George will be able to do,' I told her bleakly.

She was silent for a moment. 'Don't make pre-judgments Harry,' she said.

I nodded as if she could see me. 'Okay I won't,' I said.

'Good-bye, Harry.'

'Good-bye, Selena,' I said. We hung up and I thought about her eyes. Then I thought about Julie and remembered the man with the Viva she had been with when I called at her house. It didn't have anything to do with me, but I didn't let that stop me. I telephoned my friend at the licensing office and he told me he would ring me back. He was faster than the previous time. The computer at Swansea must have been having a good day. He told me the car was registered in the name of a food company that had its name plastered over one in every four of the advertisements I seemed to see every time I stayed in to watch television with Stanley.

I hoisted the appropriate section of the London telephone directory on to the desk, and leafed through it. I dialled the number of their head office and asked for personnel. I put on my best voice and told them I was with a building society. I gave them the name of one with even more assets than they had themselves. There's nothing like money for impressing people. It dulls their senses. I told them a lot of crap about Paul Jackson wanting a mortgage and that our formal questionnaire would be in the post, but in the meantime could they confirm that all was well, as I wanted to get things moving right away because the house he wanted to buy was being chased by someone else. I almost believed it myself, and the bird-brain at the other end of the line certainly did. He told me all the things I didn't really want to know plus the one most important thing I thought I did want to know. Until I heard it, that was. I walked over and looked out of the window but there was nothing there to inspire me. It still wasn't my business. I picked up the telephone and called the branch office of the food company where the personnel officer had told me Paul Jackson worked. I was lucky, if that's the word I want; he was there. I didn't waste time with niceties.

'I'm a friend of Julie's,' I said, which wasn't true; not after that call I wasn't. 'Don't say anything. I just want to tell you something. If Julie knows you're married, fine, that's the end of it. But if she doesn't know, then you're in trouble. Do I need to repeat any of that?' He said no and I hung up. Morgan's good deed for the day. If it was, why did I feel so rotten as I walked down the stairs? Maybe it was the bang on the head.

CHAPTER THIRTEEN

Kusborski didn't ring me that night at the Cyder House but he did the following night – from New York. I was beginning to feel lonely. I told him what I had found on the motorway site, and it didn't seem to worry him too much. The next day my War Office friend rang and told me the information I wanted would take about a week or ten days to arrive, and so I phoned Selena Cantrell and told her that I hoped to be able to identify the skeleton for her in about ten days' time. She sounded pleased about that, but her pleasure diminished when I told her what I planned to do next. That surprised me.

I talked to my estate agent friend again, and he agreed to let me view Tree Cottage, although he sounded as if he was tiring of my little game. He insisted on going with me and we went in his car. I wandered around the house and then, leaving him inside, I went out into the garden. I didn't find what I was looking for, and so I went through the shrubbery to where the garden bordered the garden of the next house. There were two piles of bricks and half a dozen sacks of cement and a pile of sand. Everything was covered in sheets of opaque plastic. I let my friend take me back to town and I rang Peters from the office.

I was just thinking of packing up and going home for the day when he finally called back.

'Come to the office,' he said.

'Did it match?' I asked.

'Come to the office,' he repeated as if he didn't hear my question. I guessed it had matched. He was sitting at his desk playing steeples with his fingers again.

'Tell me the story,' he said. 'And this time try to stay fairly close to the truth.'

'Did it match?' I asked again.

'Yes it did. The sheet around the body was cut from one of the pieces covering the building materials. Now tell me the story.' So I did.

'I was hired to find the identity of the skeleton,' I said. 'While I was digging around, someone searched my place. I guessed that they were looking for the same thing as Kusborski, and I decided to try and find out who they were. I asked around in the village and found out that two men, Americans, were looking for me. I started to make inquiries at hotels in the area. Also I put out feelers about any Americans renting houses in the district. There were lots of them, hotel residents and renters. I was following up an address I'd been given when I happened to pass Bennett's End, saw what looked like a burglary in progress and interfered. Someone hit me from behind. You know what happened next.' It wasn't the truth but it had enough of the truth in it to make it sound convincing – well, fairly convincing. Anyway he'd said himself I should stay *fairly* close to the truth.

'Who were the two men?' he asked.

'I don't know,' I said. 'But neither of the descriptions I got fitted the man I found on the motorway site.'

'Mason.'

'Mason?'

'His name was John Mason. He was a New York lawyer. Do you know a woman called Selena Cantrell?' Peters went on. I was expecting the question.

'No. Who is she?'

'A friend of Mason's.'

'She identified him for you, did she?'

He looked at me carefully. 'No she didn't. She left the country the day you found the body.'

'Oh,' I said. He stopped playing steeples and tapped his fingers furiously on the desk. I preferred the steeples.

'Okay, let's have a description of the two men who were looking for you,' Peters said. I took my time and did it right, and he sent for the Photo-fit kit, and we played jig-saw puzzles with that for a while. At the end he had two very good pictures of Alda and Martinelli.

'Okay,' Peters said. 'We'll see what we come up with. One more thing, the name of your client?'

'You know I'm not likely to give that to you.'

'Not likely, maybe, but there are no rules.'

'There are my rules.'

He looked at me and then shrugged. The shrug said he wasn't giving up, just letting it slide for the moment. 'Go back to your office and wait there until I ring you,' he said.

'Have I earned a piece of information?' I asked.

'What?'

'The house where I was found after I'd been knocked out. Bennett's End.'

'What about it?'

'Was the burglar alarm ringing?'

'Yes. That's how the owner found you.'

'What started it ringing?' I asked. He looked at me curiously.

'Someone broke a pane of glass in one of the ground-floor windows.'

'Thanks,' I said.

'What was all that about?'

'I don't know,' I told him. Well, once you start lying to the police, an extra one every now and again doesn't matter very much. I went back to the office and rang Kusborski.

'I've thrown Alda and Martinelli to the wolves,' I said.

'Why?' he asked.

'As the man said, it seemed like a good idea at the time.' I hung up.

I didn't take too seriously Inspector Peters's instruction to stay in my office until he rang me, which was just as well. It was a week before the call came.

'I thought you might like to know we've identified the two men you described to us,' he said when I walked into his office.

'Who are they?' I asked, just to keep the deception rolling.

'Mario Alda and Nicola Martinelli. Americans as you said. They are both from New York and the NYPD have long sheets on them.'

'We seem to let anyone into the country these days,' I said conversationally.

'Yes, well, New York have been talking to them. It seems they have an alibi that puts them somewhere else the night Mason was killed.'

'But I saw them.'

'So you did. Kusborski seems to think their alibi will stand up. They claim they were with a man named Alexander Merrit, an American over here on a business trip. Apparently he's a respectable citizen, a building contractor in New York, friend of the Mayor and the State Governor. Kusborski thinks Merrit will be believed and you won't. If it was brought to court, that is.'

'And who will be believed if it isn't brought to court?' I asked.

Peters hesitated and looked at me carefully. 'Kusborski seems to think that Merrit will say anything he is told to say by the man Alda and Martinelli work for.'

'Who's that?'

'A man called Capelli, Frank Capelli. Heard of him?'

'No,' I said.

Peters nodded as if I had said what I was expected to say. 'Kusborski has also identified the skeleton for us.'

I looked at him, surprised. 'Who was it?'

'A man called Capelli. Brother of Frank. This one was called Antonio. He was here as a soldier during the war. It was thought that he had died in a plane crash. Seems he didn't. There were survivors and he must have been one. Probably took advantage of the crash to desert. Pity we can't find out how he died.'

I was thinking fast and I wasn't getting anywhere. 'How did Kusborski identify him?' I asked.

'From his army records.' Peters stood up and took a file from a shelf behind his desk. He opened it and slid out a sheet and passed it to me. It was from the pathologist's report on the skeleton. 'The dental work done on the skeleton was very extensive: several fillings, cappings and also some bridgework. It is identical to the US Army's medical records on Antonio Capelli.' I looked at the document in front of me. He was right; Tony Capelli hadn't had a good tooth in his head.

'So now what happens?' I asked.

'Nothing happens. The skeleton has been identified, which ties up a loose end. We have no idea how he died so there's no point in pursuing matters here. Anyway, what could we find out after all these years?'

'What about Mason?'

'We believe your story. Almost certainly Alda and Martinelli were involved, but we can't prove it. They were probably here because their boss, Frank Capelli, sent them here to see what they could find out about his brother. They presumably met Mason and, well, who knows? They were criminals and he was a lawyer, apparently a straight one, but maybe they had an old score to settle. Anyway Kusborski seems to think he will catch up with them one day.'

'So nothing happens?'

'That's right. Nothing happens.'

'The cases are closed?' I asked.

Peters shook his head gently. 'Not exactly, but we are no longer working on them.'

'Oh,' I said. It seemed to be all there was to say.

'As for you, Mr Morgan, I think you should tread a little more carefully in the future. It will be in everyone's interest if you do.'

I stood up. 'Yes,' I said. 'In future I will be very careful what I do.' I walked out of his office and into the street. It was bright and sunny and all the girls in their summer dresses were walking past, and I felt depression coming on. I called in at the bank and got them to ask the computer for my current balance. It wasn't very impressive. I walked back up to my office, trying to work out ways I could scrape together enough money to take Stanley and me on holiday. I hadn't thought of any when I reached the building that contained my one-room self-torture chamber. I thought about going home instead, but that wouldn't have helped. I went upstairs and sat at my desk and tried to find something cheerful to think about. There was a clatter of feet on the stairs and the postman came into view with the midday delivery. He had two letters for me. I opened the airmail envelope first. There were two pieces of paper inside. One was a letter from Selena. She said she knew about the identification of the skeleton and that therefore the case was closed. She thanked me for all my help, and her boss George Capelli thanked me; and then I unfolded the other piece of paper and the First National Bank of America thanked me. It was a cheque for three thousand dollars. It looked as if Stanley and I would get a holiday after all. Then I opened the other envelope. It was from my friend at the War Office. Inside was a photocopy of Antonio Capelli's army records.

Attached to the front was a little note: 'read and destroy'. Afterwards I sat holding my head in my hands. I didn't know what to do next. One thing was certain though. The holiday would have to be postponed.

CHAPTER FOURTEEN

I wrote a polite little thank-you note to Selena and added that with any amount of luck I might earn the money she had sent me before long. Then I rang my friend at the War Office and offered to buy him lunch the next day. He accepted cautiously. We arranged to meet at a Chinese restaurant just off Tottenham Court Road. He said he would be in civilian clothes. I think he wanted to tell me he would be wearing something for me to identify him by, but I reminded him that I had known him before he wore a uniform and he laughed selfconsciously. He really had been seeing too many spy movies.

Then I had nothing to do, so I rang Michael Silver and asked him how he was doing in the quest for my thirty pounds. He said he wasn't doing very well, and with the largesse induced by the unexpected arrival of food parcels from the States, I told him to drop it. He sounded relieved and disappointed at the same time. Ten minutes after we had hung up Rosemary phoned me. Obviously the office jungle telegraph was in working order.

'How are you?' she asked. I remembered that the last time I had spoken to her had been just after my bump on the head. It seemed a very long time ago.

'Recovered,' I told her.

'You said you would ring me,' she said.

'I'm sorry,' I told her. 'I've been very busy working on a

case. It didn't leave me with any spare time. What are you doing tonight?' She said she wasn't doing anything, and I arranged to pick her up about seven. Before I went home I rang the Chez Jean and reserved a table for nine o'clock.

When Stanley came in from the site I was shaving. He came and stood by the bathroom door and I told him I was going out and would be late, and that I would get his dinner ready before I went out. He smiled cheerfully at me and we talked about nothing in particular. Talking to Stanley was never very easy, although the years had of necessity directed me into certain pre-set areas where conversation was possible without too great a struggle on either side. There was his collection, of course, and there were birds, although on that subject he had to do all the talking, while I just listened and made occasional noises to show I wasn't asleep. There were cars and engines, and although I didn't know much about either I had picked up enough over the years to hold my own. Well, when you spend a lot of time in bars you learn about cars. Men in pubs seem to talk of little else except, possibly, women. And women was one subject that Stanley never talked about, which was why it was such a surprise when he asked me about Selena.

'Have you seen the lady who was here that night?'

'No,' I said.

'She was pretty,' he said.

'Yes,' I said. 'She was.'

'That was her husband who was found on the site wasn't it?' I looked at him carefully and then rinsed my razor under the tap while I thought about the question.

'Yes,' I said eventually. 'Yes, it was. How did you know?'

'I recognized the photograph the policeman showed me.'

'Which policeman?'

'When they were asking everybody questions. They showed everyone the picture and they asked us if we had seen him before.'

I took a deep breath. 'And what did you say?'

'I didn't say anything, Harry.'

I looked at him curiously. 'Why not Stanley?'

The smile turned into a bashful grin. 'I didn't like the policeman who asked me the question, and anyway I thought maybe you didn't want anyone to know he had been here.' I looked at him in amazement.

'That's right, Stanley.' Then I thought better of it. Stanley was too uncomplicated to carry lies successfully. 'If they ask again, always tell the truth.' That salved my conscience without getting me into more hot water with the police. 'Who was the policeman who asked you? The one you didn't like?'

'His name was Fowler. He was nasty. He had a funny smile on his face all the time he was talking to me.' I grinned to myself. Sergeant Fowler's sneer had bounced back at him. I wondered what would have happened if Peters had asked the question of Stanley. That would have probably produced a different answer, and God knows what it would have done to the careful card-castle of lies I had built up. I put on a clean shirt and made Stanley's dinner. I left him contentedly eating it in front of the television set. The settee was sagging more than ever and I made a mental note to look at the salerooms in case there was anything that was going cheap. Well, even three thousand dollars wouldn't last forever.

I picked up Rosemary at her house. She must have been watching for my arrival, as she came out as I drove up. Apparently I wasn't yet ready for parental examination. I took the Horsham road out of town and told her tales of daring featuring the famous detective Harry Morgan. She seemed to enjoy them and I didn't tell too many lies. Conversation was surprisingly easy with her, and by the time we had consumed a couple of drinks in the small bar of the Chez Jean the party spirit was in full swing. I ordered a lavish meal; I don't know why I was treating her so generously – guilt complex maybe. When we were told our table was ready, we walked through into the restaurant and all the party spirit evaporated. One of the waitresses was Julie. I managed to get through the meal although I felt like doing anything but eat. Rosemary didn't seem to notice anything was amiss. As for Julie, after the first surprised glance she behaved as if she had never seen me before in her life. I looked at her closely, whenever I got the chance, and her eyes were slightly discoloured. The whites were not as white as they usually were. It didn't necessarily mean that she had been crying, but the chances were that that was the cause. As for the cause for crying, I expect that was me and my clever call to the man from the food company. When the meal was over Rosemary went off to the ladies' room and Julie came over to clear the table.

'How are you?' I asked hesitantly.

'Surviving,' she said.

'Good,' I said. 'Er, the . . .' I searched around for words where words had once come so easily.

'Is she a client?' Julie asked, giving me an opportunity to take the easy way out.

'Yes,' I said. 'I'm looking for her mother and father and . . . Oh Christ, Julie, I didn't know you would be here.'

'I know you didn't. Two of their regular girls are ill and they had to take on temporary staff in a hurry. The agency gave them my number, and, well, it's all money isn't it? Anyway why shouldn't you be here? I don't have any priority, Harry.' I nodded, trying to find some way to ask if Paul Jackson was still calling, but I couldn't. Not without giving away my involvement. I saw Rosemary coming back.

'Can I ring you?' I asked, and as I saw the refusal forming on her lips I added, 'Just to talk.' She nodded and went away as Rosemary sat down. I smiled brightly and falsely and paid the bill and we left.

I drove back towards the town and eventually my preoccupation registered.

'Is anything wrong?' Rosemary asked.

'No, I'm sorry. Did you enjoy your dinner?'

'Yes, marvellous. I've never been there before. Was it expensive?' It seemed an odd thing to say but I put it down to youth.

'Not really,' I said. 'We can't go back to the cottage,' I added. 'My cousin will be there. And, well, we can't go back there.'

'Oh.' She seemed disappointed. 'We can't go to my house because Mummy and Daddy will be there.' I can't stand women who use words like mummy and daddy but I gritted my teeth. I was going off Rosemary.

'We'll go for a drive instead,' I told her.

'Don't use too much petrol, not at the price it is,' she said. I was irritated by the second hint of concern at my habits of expenditure.

'Don't worry about what I do with my money,' I said brusquely.

'Oh, I'm not interfering, Harry,' she said. 'It's just that I don't want you to waste money on me now.' I started to make a joke about it being all right if I wasted money on her later, when the implication registered – she was hearing wedding-bells. I was no longer going off her. I had gone off her completely. With the rest of the evening to get through I thought rapidly, and decided to take her for a long, tiring walk. That would keep her quiet for the night and after that I would be safe. I increased speed and drove through the town and up past St Luke's hospital, and eventually reached the car park at the foot of the hill that led to St Martha's church. The walk up the hill didn't do me very much good, and I was doing my best not to gasp too loudly for breath when we reached the top. It was a warm night and it was clear and bright under the moon and stars, and I realised my mistake as soon as we were there.

'Oh, Harry, it's so romantic here,' she whispered and I have to admit that she was right. It was quiet and peaceful, no sounds of life, and the only signs of it were the lights of cars in the valley below, moving along the Shalford road. She put her arms around me and kissed me and I didn't fight her off. Then she became more insistent, and although there was no one there to see I took her hand and led her back among the trees. I hadn't made love to anyone in the open air for twenty years and I had forgotten how enjoyable it could be.

Afterwards I took her home and she sat with her head on my shoulder all the way there, singing something I didn't recognise but took to be a currently popular song. I stopped outside her door.

'Do you want to come in for coffee?' she asked.

'Your parents are still up,' I said pointing at the lighted windows.

'That doesn't matter,' she said. It does to me, I thought.

'Perhaps another time,' I said. She seemed disappointed but she didn't argue. We said good night and I kissed her in a way I hoped she would remember after she had got over the fact that she wouldn't be seeing me again. Then I went home to bed.

CHAPTER FIFTEEN

My friend from the War Office was a captain and his name was Dominic Jervoise-Clarke. He suited the name in his appearance and in his job. With a name like that he almost had to go into the army and almost certainly he had to rise to a very high rank. No one ever heard of a private called Jervoise-Clarke did they? I had met him when Stanley and I were still bumming around the country, trying to scrape a living. Stanley had been working part-time at a garage and Dominic had brought his XK Jaguar in for service, and it was the first high-performance car Stanley had ever worked on. He made it go better than it had ever gone before and Dominic was delighted. He brought his father's Rolls, and Stanley did his stuff with that, and then there was a succession of sports cars belonging to friends of Dominic, and then he had found how much the garage owner was paying Stanley, and he had shown himself to be anything but a chinless wonder. He had told the man what he thought of him, and he tried to set up Stanley and me with a little garage of our own except, of course, I was too bloody-minded to want to sit in one place keeping accounts and doing as Stanley told me. So we didn't do it, but I was left with an odd sort of respect for the man. He was about nineteen then and he joined the army a year later and seemed to do very well, very quickly. Of all the people I've met there are very few with whom I have kept in touch, and of them all Dominic was the least likely to have remained a friend. But he had. I liked him and, surprisingly enough, he liked me. He certainly liked Stanley, and as for Stanley, I think he came close to worshipping Dominic Jervoise-Clarke.

The Chinese restaurant was dark and suitably inscrutable. The waiters moved about softly making hissing noises that passed for speech, and from time to time they deigned to serve their customers. The food was exceptionally good. Talking intelligibly over a Chinese meal is sometimes difficult to the point of being impossible. I therefore waited until we had reached the sweet before I raised the matter that had prompted the meeting. Dominic was spooning up lychees and looking for all the world like a slightly overgrown schoolboy up from the country on a day trip. He had large brown eyes set in the middle of a round red face that seemed to be in a permanent state of mild surprise. I put a spoonful of crystallised fruits into my mouth, and as I chewed on them I took the papers he had sent me out of my pocket. His eyes went bigger and rounder and he almost choked on his lychees.

'I thought I told you to read and destroy them,' he spluttered.

'Calm down, laddie,' I told him. 'I have taken a photocopy of the part I'm interested in, and you can take this back and destroy it yourself to set your mind at rest.' He snatched the papers from my hand and pushed them hastily into his inside jacket pocket.

'Bloody idiot,' he said. After he had calmed down a fraction his curiosity got the better of him. 'What's it all about?'

'I'm not sure,' I told him. 'But I think your friend in the Pentagon, or wherever he is, might be able to help unravel the problem if he will.'

'Is it another unclassified matter like this one?'

'I can't think why not.'

He finished off the last of his lychees and put down his spoon. 'Okay, ask away.'

'Towards the end of 1943, August 23rd to be exact, an American Army-Air Force Dakota took off from Dunsfold in Surrey. It crashed on take-off and almost everyone on board was killed. There were five survivors. I want their names and their last known addresses.'

'Is that all?' he asked me.

'Yes.'

'Okay, Harry, I'll see what I can do, even if I end up being reduced to the ranks.'

'That won't happen, Dominic. The army needs all the Jervoise-Clarkes it can get.'

'I expect you're right,' he said with mock humility. 'I say, do you suppose I could have some more of those lychees?' I waved to the waiter and after several minutes he deigned to notice the foreign white devil and came across to take our order.

After I had said good-bye to Dominic, and he had marched stiffly off back to the War Office, I decided not to waste the train fare by going back too soon. I went to the address I had found for the lady from Devon's daughter – motto of the firm, we never let go. At least not where there's money at stake. The address turned out to be a seedy flat in a very seedy house in an even seedier street. The girl was in and she looked frightened to death when I told her who I was, but I impressed on her that I just wanted to talk. She invited me in. The flat was one room; there was a carpet of sorts on the floor, and the furniture, what there was of it, would have been broken up for firewood in most homes. In fact some of it looked as if someone had started doing that already. There was a bed and a table with a bright orange plastic laminated top. Two chairs, one in matching bright orange and one, by way of contrast, in bright blue. There was one armchair with its bottom hanging out, and inevitably there was a television set.

'You didn't go home with your mother,' I said.

'No, I didn't.' She had a quiet, pleasant voice. She didn't look like the type who would run away from home and join the army, if there is a type for either of those acts.

'Why not?'

'She didn't seem to want to change.'

'Change?'

'She thinks she owns me.'

'Mothers often do,' I said. She looked at me and then managed a small smile.

'Yes, I suppose I'm not saying anything original.'

'Are you living here alone?' I asked. She looked at me with a flash of anger and then it died, and she started to cry softly. I sat there and let her. After a while she stopped and looked at me defiantly.

'Yes, I am alone,' she said.

'Why did he leave you?'

'Someone else.'

'Can you manage?'

'Not really. It would be better if I could find someone to share, but there isn't really room for two unless—' she hesitated, 'unless you share everything, and I don't want to do that.' What she seemed to be telling me was that she wasn't promiscuous. She seemed to think that she had to defend herself. That's what some people are driven to do these days, defending themselves for behaving in a way that a generation ago was accepted as being the only way to behave.

'You could go home,' I said. 'On your terms, of course.'

'What terms?'

'Oh, I don't know. Stay at home for a couple of weeks maybe while you look for a flat nearby. Your mother lives at Crediton. That's near Exeter, isn't it?'

'Yes.'

'Well there must be jobs there – and flats, probably big enough to share with another girl. You could see your mother at week-ends and she could visit you. It could work.'

'It could,' she seemed to want to believe it.

'It's called compromise,' I said.

She smiled and then the smile faded.

'I can't.'

'Why not?'

'I owe two weeks rent here and then there's the train fare home.'

'I'll pay,' I said. 'You can send me the money when you get a job.' She looked at me for a moment.

'Why are you doing this?' she asked.

I grinned at her. 'When you didn't go home your mother refused to pay my bill, so you could say I was doing it for the money.'

She looked at me and after a moment she laughed.

I paid the landlord the rent she owed and I took her to the station. I bought her ticket and a magazine to read on the train, and I gave her enough money to get a taxi home. After I had seen the train off I went into a telephone box and rang her mother. She almost hung up on me, but I stopped her and I told her what had happened and what time the train was due in. I told her that if she said one thing out of place her daughter would very likely be on the first train back to London. She started to thank me and I interrupted and said there was only one way I wanted thanking, and hung up. I took the tube to Waterloo and caught the train back to Guildford. I felt extremely virtuous.

CHAPTER SIXTEEN

Virtue is its own reward, the saying goes. Maybe, but my good deed with the young lady from Devon certainly started a week of inquiries. I took on three jobs: one I farmed out to an agency in Liverpool, taking care to add a comfortable percentage on the top for me, and the other two kept me active around the area. One of them was another missing person, and the other was a small jewellery theft following a party where all the guests had been friends or relatives. My client thought that the police might tread on too many toes. By the end of the week I had found the missing person, and instead of making the mistake I had made with the lady in Devon I made sure I collected my fee before I traded the address. I also recovered the jewellery and took it back to the owner, who thanked me profusely and refused to let me tell him the name of the person who had taken it. He also paid up without hesitation and so the bank balance was flourishing. On the Friday afternoon Selena rang me from New York.

'What was your cryptic message supposed to mean?' she asked.

'It meant what it said. I'm planning to earn my fee any day now.'

'That was to repay you for keeping me out of things when John was . . . died.'

'I did that because you have beautiful eyes,' I said.

'Don't be ridiculous, Mr Morgan,' she snapped. I wondered where the Harry had gone, and then it occurred to me that she might not be alone.

'All right, I did that because, as far as I could see, you had nothing to do with his death and nothing would be gained by involving you.'

'Thank you,' she said. 'I still don't see what you are doing working on the case.'

'Doesn't George want to know what happened to his brother Tony?' I asked. There was silence and I listened to the static again. I seemed to be doing that a lot; it was replacing staring at walls as my favourite occupation.

'Tony died. No one can find out after all this time how he died,' Selena said.

'Who said he's dead?' I asked.

'Who . . .? The skeleton – the police obtained a report from the army. It showed that the skeleton was that of Tony Capelli.'

'So they did,' I said cheerfully.

'What are you saying?' she asked.

'What do you think I'm saying?' I asked.

'I . . ' There was silence again.

'Are you still there?' I asked after a moment.

'Yes.' Her voice was fainter, as if she was further from the telephone. I had the impression that someone else was listening to the instrument with her.

'I have a message for George,' I said. 'Tell him that I don't know whether his brother is alive or dead. After all this time I expect that he is very probably dead. I don't much care either way, but one thing I do know. The skeleton Stanley found was not the skeleton of Tony Capelli.' There was silence again and then a man's voice, deep and rasping as if he had an inflamed throat.

'Mr Morgan, this is George Capelli. You are certain that what you have just said is true?'

'Yes, I am.'

'Then perhaps my brother died in the plane crash after all.'

'Perhaps he did.'

'Then why are you expressing doubts?'

'If he did die in the crash, why is someone going to a lot of trouble to prove that he died in a wood in Surrey?' I asked. He was silent for a moment. When he spoke again the gravelly voice was brisk and hard.

'Very well, Mr Morgan. What Miss Cantrell told you a moment ago is so. The cheque she sent you was to thank you for protecting her. I would like to hire your services. Find out whatever you can about my brother Tony. Find out if he's alive or dead; and if he is dead, how he died.' The voice dropped lower. 'And if he was murdered, find who murdered him.'

'It was a very long time ago, Mr Capelli,' I said.

'Time has nothing to do with it, Mr Morgan,' he said. 'Do you accept?'

'I'll do what I can,' I said. I waited a moment and Selena came back on the line.

'If it becomes necessary for me to come to England, will the police want to question me?'

'Probably not, but we'll cross that bridge if we come to it. Anyway, why do you think it might be necessary for you to come to England?'

'Mr Capelli thinks you may need assistance.'

I thought for a moment. 'Mr Capelli might be right,' I said. 'But if he is, I expect I can find the assistance I need right here.'

'Perhaps,' she said. 'If you change your mind, you have my number.'

'Yes,' I said. 'I have your number.'

Late in the afternoon Dominic Jervoise-Clarke telephoned me and said he had what I wanted. He said he would post it to me, but I was eager to see what he had and, as the next day was Saturday and it was therefore unlikely that the post would reach me before Monday, I said I would drive up the following morning if that would not inconvenience him. He said it wouldn't and suggested we meet in Regent's Park Zoo. He was taking things too far and I decided I would have to talk to him seriously about his attempts at subterfuge. We arranged to meet at the gorilla's cage. I went home and told Stanley I was going to the zoo and I asked him if he would like to come too. It was like offering a small boy a lifetime's supply of sweets and ice-cream.

Stanley and I reached the zoo a couple of hours before the time Dominic had set for our meeting. I don't know what it is about zoos. I like seeing the animals and there, in Regent's Park, they look well-fed and healthy and I have no doubt they are better off than in the wilds. But it doesn't alter the fact that I feel sorry for them. Stanley, of course, had no such problems; he enjoyed every moment of the time we were there, and he was only slightly put out when midday arrived and I turned our steps towards the gorilla. Stanley liked the gorilla best of all. I didn't. He imparted to me a strange sense of unease. It seemed as if the cage was there as a token only, and that if he wanted he could tear it apart with all the effort a tiger would need to open a canary's cage.

Stanley stood looking at the gorilla and the gorilla looked at Stanley. There seemed to be an element of mutual respect and admiration in their eyes. I wouldn't have given odds on either of them in a fight. Mark you, if gorillas are as amiable as their opponents claim them to be, then starting a fight between the two of them would have been as easy as lighting a wet newspaper with a damp match.

Dominic arrived exactly on time. He could never do otherwise. He greeted Stanley with all the charm and courtesy he always displayed, and they talked animatedly for some time about motorcars. It seemed that Dominic was currently running a Lotus and he extolled its virtues to Stanley, ending with a sigh of regret that his present garage mechanic was somewhat lower in the scale of things than Stanley. I took the hint; as I've said before nobody does things for nothing any more. I arranged to take Stanley to Dominic's one week-end and let him work on the car. I didn't mind. Dominic was taking risks, giving me information I couldn't get for myself. Not that it was classified – I had told him the truth – but it wasn't what he was supposed to do. He had the names and addresses written down on a piece of paper. His handwriting was neat and flowery. There were four names and addresses.

'What happened to the fifth?' I asked.

'He died later on in the war. In France.'

I nodded. It reduced my chances from slim to slight. I slipped the paper in my pocket, and the three of us wandered around for another hour before I felt justified in spoiling Stanley's day for him by taking him home. I said good-bye to Dominic, then Stanley and I walked back to the main entrance, leaving him standing watching the seals lazing in the sun. He looked slightly ludicrous in his cavalry-twill trousers and dogstooth check jacket and his neat little pork-pie hat. Absurdly, I felt sorry for him. I think the three hours spent looking at the caged animals had softened me up.

I went straight to the office, telling Stanley I wanted to make some telephone calls. I asked him if he wanted to come up and he almost exploded with pleasure. The zoo and now my tatty office in one day were almost too much for him. I looked at him as he walked beside me from the car park. I wondered why I had never thought to take him to the office before. He sat in the other chair, carefully motionless so that it didn't disintegrate beneath him. I dialled the international directory operator and eventually I had telephone numbers for all four of the ex-army men on Dominic's list. They were well scattered throughout the States and all were in small towns, so none of them could be reached by direct dialling. I did a little sum, and with the help of a diagram I eventually came to the conclusion that it was well before breakfast there; in the case of one of the addresses on the West Coast it would be well before dawn. I wanted co-operation so I reluctantly decided to be patient.

I took Stanley home and made a meal for us. After we had eaten I left him watching a Western on TV; it was *Stage Coach*, not the original, the re-make. There should be a law against re-making motion pictures. I drove back to the office and dialled the operator and gave her one of the numbers on the list. I picked the one on the East Coast, intending to travel westwards in the hope that none of the men on the list were planning on sleeping late.

The first man was in, and the operator connected us. Fortunately it was a clear line and I was able to explain who I was and what I wanted. I had devised a cover story: that I had been retained by a firm of lawyers to look into the possible existence of an illegitimate child of Tony Capelli, who might be heir to a considerable sum of money. It didn't convince me, but then I'd invented it, yet it had all the ingredients that would allow most people to open up with a reasonably easy conscience. Always assuming they had something to open up about. I got nowhere with the first man. He remembered Capelli, in fact I had to stop him reeling off the names of all forty men in the outfit, but he hadn't known him as a friend. He sounded like one of those people who organise army reunions, great on events and statistics but rotten when it came to the human beings involved. The second man was out when I rang, and I left my number with the promise that I would pay for the call if he called me back, and that if I didn't hear within a couple of days I would ring him again. On the third call I found myself talking to a bitter, deserted wife. She didn't know where her husband had gone and she didn't care, and who the hell was

I anyway to call her up in the middle of the night. I hung up in a hurry and recalculated the time difference. I came up with the same answer as before. She must have had a hard night. With only one call to make, I realised I was getting close to the bottom of the barrel and I searched through the desk drawers for the whisky bottle. It wasn't there and after a moment's thought I tried the filing cabinet. Kusborski must have had a sense of humour after all; it was filed under W. I poured a small measure and dialled the operator and asked for the last number. I replaced the receiver and immediately it rang. It was a different operator; the second man was calling me back and would I pay for the call; I said I would, and would she ask her colleague to hold the call I had just placed until later. She said she would, and connected me.

Chris Condoli lived in Abingdon, Virginia and he sounded friendly all the way up to where I told him my cover story. Then he changed.

'Okay, mister,' he said. 'That's the story for the mugs, now tell me what you really want?' I thought rapidly and then decided that he must know something I didn't, and if I was to persuade him to tell me what it was, I needed his confidence.

'I'm sorry, Mr Condoli. You're right, that was just a cover story. I needed that to keep the real facts from anyone who didn't know Tony Capelli well. Can I take it you were a friend of his?'

'You can,' he said. He sounded slightly less cold.

'Right. The truth is that a body has been found here in England. A body that has been there for over thirty years, and fake evidence had been planted with it to make the police believe it was the body of a man called D'Angelo. It was soon found that the man wasn't D'Angelo, but we still didn't know who it was. Then more evidence turned up, and this time it identified the body as that of Tony Capelli.'

'You're kidding?'

'No I'm not, but I know that it wasn't Tony. But that still leaves me with a lot of unanswered questions. One is what really happened to Tony, and another is why is someone trying to make out he didn't die in the crash.'

'I can't help you with the second question, Mr Morgan, but as for the first, there's no doubt at all – Tony was in the crash.'

'You're sure?'

'Sure I'm sure.'

'I would appreciate it if you could tell me everything you can remember about Tony and about the hours before the crash.'

'Okay, Mr Morgan, if it will help straighten up whatever is going on. You know Tony wasn't the kind of guy people took him to be. Most of the guys, well, they thought he was a hood. Because of his father you know. And I have to admit I thought the same at first. That was when we were over here in the States.'

'Tell me about the time you met Tony, Mr Condoli.'

'Call me Chris, Harry.'

'Okay, Chris. Tell me what happened. Did you meet before or after the formation of the special squad?'

'After. I don't think any of the guys knew one another before. I was told about the squad by my company commander. He'd had a directive that any men of Italian descent were to be asked to volunteer for a special squad. I volunteered. They gave me some tests at my own camp first—'

'What kind of tests?' I interrupted.

'Mainly intelligence tests – I guess they didn't want any dummies – and they also tested how good my Italian was. They were very careful with that test. They wanted to be sure that I spoke it without too much of an accent. Too much of an American accent, that is. Then, when they were happy with that, I was shipped out to a training camp near here.'

'Here?'

'Abingdon, Virginia. That's why I live here now. I met a girl here and after the war I came back, married and stayed. We have two kids. Of course, they're grown up now. Joseph, he's the eldest, is a doctor, fine boy. Pete, he's doing real well too; he's in Detroit working with General Motors. He's an executive V.P.'

'Great, just fine,' I said, hoping to bring him back to the matter in hand.

'Yeah, anyway,' Condoli went on, 'we all met here for the first time. About fifty of us. We started some real intensive training, and by the time we were through we were down to forty men. All fit and all bright and all raring to go.'

'What was Tony Capelli like, then?'

'He was quiet, you know. Never said anything out of place, but most of the other guys kept out of his way. But I kind of liked him, you know. Then just before we moved out of Abingdon there was a little bit of trouble, nothing much, just a fight with another outfit. We'd all had too much to drink, I guess, and Tony, well, he turned out to be a real regular guy in a fight. After that the three of us stayed together a lot.'

'The three of you?'

'Yes. Me, Tony and Gerry Brown. We got real friendly, you know. And after we got to England we always kept together. Did all our training and eating and drinking together.' Over the thousands of miles between us I heard Chris Condoli give an embarrassed laugh. 'They called us the Three Musketeers. The other guys, you know.'

'What kind of a man was Tony, when you really knew him?'

'He was quiet and he thought a lot and he was always reading books.'

'What kind of books?'

'The kind none of the other guys read – real heavy stuff, classics, that kind of thing. And all your writers, Shakespeare and Dickens, you know.'

'Did you go out much – around the area?'

'Not much, not at first. We were only there a few months, but Tony met this girl and he started seeing her every opportunity he could get. We used to rib him about it, but he never took offence. He was serious about her, no doubt about it. That's why I knew he didn't leave an illegitimate kid. He wouldn't have done that, not Tony. He was serious about Mary.'

'Mary?'

'Mary Graham, that was her name. She worked in the canteen at Pirbright where we were stationed.'

'What happened the day of the crash?'

'Well, we were expecting to be mobilised any day, but when the orders came they caught us on the hop. Half the guys were out of the barracks. The MPs had to round them up in a hurry. I was in camp that night and they sent me out to help them collect the guys.'

'What about Tony?'

'Tony and Gerry had gone out together. I'd stayed behind to write to Carrie, that's my wife. Anyway while I was out helping the MPs, Tony and Gerry must have come back in, because they were there when I got back.'

'You saw Tony?'

'Sure did.' There was a moment's silence. 'Can't say I saw Gerry, but he was there because Tony said he was. Mind you, it was a long time ago.'

'Yes. Go on, Chris.'

'Well, we kitted up and moved out. They took us out to the trucks and we went to this airfield at a place called Dunsomething.'

'Dunsfold.'

'That's the place. The aircraft, it was a Dakota, was waiting and it was all warmed up and ready to go. We went on board and she taxied out for take-off.' This time the silence was longer and I knew that the man at the other end of the telephone line was re-living what was probably the worst moment of his life. 'It was one hell of a mess,' he said eventually. 'We went down the runway and I felt her lift off, then she slewed over to one side and . . . well, they said afterwards that her wing-tip dug in and she cartwheeled. I don't remember a lot about it. There was a lot of noise and a lot of shouting and then I was outside the thing. Seems the tail-section broke away aft of the doorway. That was where I was. Since then I always sit as far back in an aircraft as I can. If it happens again, maybe I'll stay lucky.'

'What happened to Tony? Where was he sitting?'

'Tony was forward of me, about three rows down, with Gerry.'

I looked at the list of names Dominic had given me. 'Where were the others sitting? Those that survived with you: Mondi, Drucci, Genite and Barasa.'

'Say, you have been doing your homework on this. Well, Mondi was sitting next to me, and Drucci and Genite were right behind me. Barasa was farther forward.'

'How far forward?'

'Two, three rows maybe.'

'Near where Tony was sitting?'

'Yes, I guess so. If you're contacting all the guys maybe you could ask him.'

'No,' I said. 'Barasa died in France.'

'Hell, maybe he wasn't as lucky as we thought we were. What about the others?'

'I haven't talked to Genite yet. Drucci's moved on from the address I had, and Mondi didn't seem to know much.'

'Mondi? No, he was always writing to me. Trying to start reunions. I told him all I wanted to do about the war was forget it. That's about all I can remember, Harry. Has it helped?'

'I think it might have done. Tell me, Chris. You saw Tony before you went on the aircraft. Did you see him on board?'

'Definitely,' he said firmly. I thought for a moment.

'What about Gerry? You said before you didn't remember seeing him at the barracks. Did you see him on the aircraft?'

'Can't say I did, but he must have been there.'

'What makes you so sure?'

'Because we had a roll call. In fact there were two, one before we left the camp and one when we boarded the aircraft.'

'Yes, that seems to make it definite. Chris, you've been a great help. Just one more thing. The girl Tony knew here, Mary Graham. You said you knew my story was phony because Tony was serious about Mary. How did you know she wasn't pregnant by him?'

'Because I would have known by looking at her.'

'You saw her after the crash?'

'Yes, she came to the hospital.'

'How often?'

'Just once, none of us, the five of us, knew her real well. She was very cut up about Tony. Then about six months later, when I got out of hospital, I went to see her, to say good-bye before they sent me back home. She wasn't pregnant then, so if she ever did get pregnant it wasn't through Tony.'

'No, you're right. Where did you go to see her?'

'At the camp at Pirbright.'

'She was still working there?'

'Yes.'

'How was she?'

'She seemed a lot better, happier, you know.'

'Was she a local girl?'

'No, she wasn't.'

'Do you know where she came from?'

'Sure do. I could hardly forget it.'

'Why not?'

'She came from a town called Abingdon. Same name as where I live now. Where we were, Tony and Gerry and me and all the guys, when we first met.'

'Thanks, Chris. One last thing. Did you ever see Tony with a gold medallion. It had a pattern on it like a rose.'

'No, not that I remember.'

'Okay, Chris, thanks a lot.'

'Call me when you know what it's all about will you?' he said.

I told him I would, and we hung up. I looked at my watch. It was a good job George Capelli was paying for the inquiry, my telephone bill was going to be colossal.

CHAPTER SEVENTEEN

Abingdon isn't a very big place – Abingdon, Berkshire that is, not Abingdon, Virginia. I've no idea whether the American town is large or small. There were only four Graham families on Abingdon's electoral roll. The second one turned out to be related to Mary Graham. Not closely related but they remembered hearing about her. The couple I spoke to were very helpful, particularly after I told my little story. I used the same one I had used before. I reckoned it would serve unless I turned up someone who knew her well enough to know it was a phoney, as Chris Condoli had done. The couple were in their late forties; the husband's father was a cousin of Mary's father. I wasn't sure what relation that made him, and he didn't seem too sure either, but I think he thought it was close enough to count if there was any money left after Mary's child had got its share. I felt almost sorry that the money didn't exist; they looked as if they could have done with it. They were helpful but they didn't know much. They had never met her. They knew she had worked away from the area in the war, but they didn't know where. That was almost all. They gave me the name of an old lady who had been a friend of all the Grahams and who, they thought, might know more. The old lady's name was Mrs Kenny, and after a long search through their old Christmas-card lists they found her address in Oxford. I drove over and found the house where the old girl lived.

Oxford had a reputation for being clean and graceful. The old lady lived in a clean and graceful house and looked as if she wouldn't see the year out. It was her first visitor for several months. Clean and graceful towns are just as heartless as dirty and ugly ones. Probably more so – in ugly, dirty towns there are no appearances to be kept up. I told her who I was and who had given me her address. She seemed to have most of her faculties left. I guessed her age at being well past ninety, and on impulse I didn't tell her my tale. I reckoned she would either see through the illegitimate child lie or, worse, believe it and go into shock. I didn't tell her all the truth. I simply told her I was trying to trace an American soldier Mary had known in the war, and it might be a help if I could talk to Mary myself.

'But Mary doesn't live here any more,' she told me.

'Not here, I know. I wondered if you have heard from her since the war,' I said.

'She wrote to me just after the war ended to tell me she was going away. After that I never heard again.'

I murmured something about being sorry, and that people were inclined to be forgetful. She didn't seem too bothered. I suppose, on balance, more people had lost contact with her than had retained it. She pointed a thin arm at the wall behind me. I looked round. It was covered in framed photographs, seemingly no two the same size.

'That one,' she said. I stood up and walked over to the wall. The one she wanted me to look at was small, a tiny blurred snapshot of a woman and a man. I lifted it down. It was too fogged to permit identification. Only one thing was clear: the man wasn't in uniform.

'This is Mary, is it?' I asked.

'Yes, that's her. Pretty girl isn't she?' Mrs Kenny said. I agreed she was. The blur could have concealed a pretty face.

'Who is the man?'

'He was the one she married,' she said.

'When?'

The old lady screwed up her face in concentration. 'She sent me the photograph with her last letter, the one where she said she was going away.'

'And she was already married then?' I asked.

'No, she said she was getting married and then they were going away.'

'Did she say where they were going?'

'Canada. No, wait a moment, was it there or was it Australia? No it was Kitty's daughter who went to Australia. Mary said she was going to Canada.'

'Did she tell you the name of the man she was going to marry?'

The old lady thought for a moment. 'No,' she said, shaking her head. 'She didn't. I think I would have remembered if she had.' I had the impression she would have done, too. Like a lot of old people her grasp of family was firm, even if other things, like the difference between Canada and Australia were a little weak.

'I don't suppose you kept her letter? That last one?' I asked her. It was a long shot and it didn't pay off.

'No, I used to keep letters but they're sad things,' she said. I looked at the photographs on the wall. They didn't seem especially cheerful but I didn't say so. I looked again at the photograph in my hand. The man and the woman were both standing upright, and there wasn't very much height difference; the man was maybe an inch or two taller. The woman's shoes were cut off in the photograph and I couldn't see therefore if she was wearing high heels or not.

'How tall was Mary?' I asked.

'Oh, she was a tiny thing, only five feet and a little bit. She always wore those high heels to make her look taller. Bad for the feet I used to tell her.'

I nodded, more to myself than to Mrs Kenny. 'Thank you,' I said. I hesitated for a moment. 'Do you think I could borrow this photograph? I'll take care of it and send it back to you.'

'Of course you can, Mr Morgan. And if you do find Mary, ask her to write to me. Please.'

I nodded again. 'Were you surprised when she didn't write?'

The old lady's eyes glistened. 'Yes, I was. I thought she would. Not the others.' She waved a dismissive hand to the wall of photographs. 'Not the others, but I thought she would.'

I left her and drove back to Guildford with the photograph of Mary Graham and the man she was to have married in my pocket, the man she was to have married after the war was over, and just before she emigrated to Canada. Or was it Australia?

From my office I rang Selena Cantrell and told her I wanted a photograph of Tony Capelli. She asked me if I had anything to report and I said I hadn't. She didn't sound very happy, but whether that was because of me and my lack of news, or for some other reason, I had no way of knowing. I sat at my desk and took the army report on Tony Capelli out of the top drawer. The one with the lock. I looked at it carefully, trying to see if there was anything I had missed. There seemed to be nothing significant. Apart from the one thing I had spotted right away the first time I had looked at it. The fact that, unlike the skeleton, and unlike the forged report that Peters had had from New York, this one gave Tony Capelli an almost perfect set of teeth. Only two fillings in fact. I picked up the telephone and called Dominic. He sounded as if he was growing a little weary of my persistence. I mentally allocated something more than a service on the Lotus by way of payment.

'Can you ask your friend for some more information? This will definitely be the last request,' I said.

'Definitely?'

'Maybe definitely.'

He sighed. 'Okay, what do you want this time?'

I told him and he said he would call me when he received it. I telephoned an agency in London and asked them to do a search for me at Somerset House, then I called Canada House and started that particular ball rolling. Just to be on the safe side I rang Australia House too. Then I went out and arranged for a photographer to make a blow-up of the photograph of Mary Graham and friend. He told me it would be ready the next day. After that I couldn't think of anything else to do, and so I went home.

I waited patiently for things to happen. Nothing much did. Apart from an expensive-looking envelope postmarked Crediton that arrived in the middle of the week. The lady from Devon had suffered a sharp attack of conscience. Her letter thanked me profusely. Her cheque covered the thirty pounds she owed me, her daughter's rail fare and a little bit over for my trouble. There was no mention of the back rent I'd paid, but I assumed the girl hadn't mentioned that part of the deal. I paid the cheque into the bank with every confidence that this time it wouldn't bounce. The next day I had a call from the London agency who gave me a negative report from Somerset House.

Three days after that the post was somewhat more exciting. Three letters, one from Selena Cantrell and one each from Canada House and Australia House. Selena's letter was short and neither friendly, nor unfriendly, just businesslike. I don't know why that disappointed me but it did. All that George Capelli had, she told me, were a few badly posed snapshots taken when Tony had been very young, but she had spoken to a friend in the morgue at the *New York Times*, and he had dug through their old records and come up with a photograph of the three brothers taken at the funeral of old Joe Capelli. The Capelli brothers were short, stocky and remarkably similar in their appearance. They looked like three pictures of the same man taken at different stages of his life. Tony was a little thinner than the others, but that was all; there was nothing to separate the blank unemotional stare that each of them directed at the camera. I pulled out the blow-up the photographic shop had done for me. The man with Mary Graham could have been Tony Capelli, or it could have been George, or it could have been Frank. For that matter it could have been almost any shortish, stocky man in his twenties or thirties. That hadn't progressed me one little bit. Mary Graham's face was clearer, but if I did find her, thirty years would have taken their toll. I thought that perhaps it had been a waste of time after all. Canada House and Australia House both said the same thing. Mary Graham hadn't emigrated to either country, either as a single or as a married woman. I seemed to have reached a dead end.

Dominic gave me a way out of the impasse. He rang me and told me he had the information I wanted. I short-circuited his complicated systems for arranging meetings and told him to meet me at Waterloo Station in an hour's time. I ran for the station and caught the first train to London. I didn't have long to wait – one advantage of living in commuter country. Dominic was standing near Smith's bookstall, hiding behind a copy of the *Daily Telegraph.* It didn't help. I recognised the trousers and the pork-pie hat. Fifteen minutes later I was on a train heading back to Guildford. I was the only man on that part of the train; the rest of the passengers were women going back to their home-made prisons after a brief escape to the big city. I sat alone in a corner and looked at the sheet on Gerald Brown. His father's name had been Bernetti, which settled one small point that had bothered me. An Italian-American named Brown had seemed a trifle incongruous. It told me two things I had wanted to know. Life seemed a little brighter.

I went back to waiting again. I seemed to be doing a lot of

that. I thought of starting a hobby, something I could do between bursts of mental strain. I came to the conclusion there was nothing that interested me very much. That started me thinking about women for no real reason I can think of. I had avoided ringing Rosemary, and after two calls to me that I had sidetracked fairly neatly she seemed to have given me up. I rang Julie and she was in. She wouldn't let me call at the house, but after a lot of pressure she did agree to meet me for a drink.

We met at the Jolly Farmer down by the river, and we sat in the garden watching the swans swim by, eyeing the bread-crust-throwing humans with all the disdain their regal association permitted. Julie's eyes had that same faint discolouration I had noticed on that last awful evening I had seen her at the Chez Jean.

'How are you?' I asked eventually.

She shrugged. Her skin looked less clear than it had been. I felt one part of me observing her in a detached manner. It was a part of me I didn't like to know existed, the cold-blooded part.

'Surviving,' she said. I had heard her say that before. It isn't an answer really. It's a way of saying things are lousy without seeming to, in case the listener doesn't want to be bothered with your troubles.

'Is survival enough?' I asked, to show that I did want to be bothered.

'It's better than nothing,' she said. I wondered if I could chance bringing up the name of the man from the food company.

'Are you still seeing, I forget the name, the man who was there that day?' I asked. She looked at me carefully.

'Paul,' she said. 'Paul Jackson. No I haven't seen him for some time.'

'Oh,' I said.

'It turned out he was married.'

'Oh,' I said again. We looked at each other, and I tried to put the thought aside that she wasn't as attractive as I had always thought she was. I kept comparing her to Selena Cantrell.

'Are you busy?' she asked.

'Yes,' I said.

'Still working on the same case?'

'The same case?'

'The girl you had with you in the restaurant,' she said. I remembered the lie I had told.

'No, not that case.'

'She was pretty.'

'Yes I suppose she was. She was also very young.'

'Too young?' she asked. I detected a slight smile in her eyes.

'Even for me,' I said.

'Take me home, Harry,' she said. I took her home, and after the babysitter had departed with carefully averted eyes, we went upstairs and we made love, and we both said how much we had missed one another, which was true for me and seemed to be true for her. We also said that our love-making had been just as good as it had always been, which wasn't true. It wasn't true at all.

CHAPTER EIGHTEEN

I telephoned Inspector Peters and asked if I could walk over and see him. He said I could if it was important. I told him it was. He was sitting at his desk examining his finger-nails as if he had never seen them before, and Sergeant Fowler was sitting squarely in a chair examining Inspector Peters with a very similar expression on his face. When he saw me he put the sneer back into place. I ignored him and sat down facing Peters without waiting to be asked. I waited until he had finished his inspection, and had satisfied himself that no one had stolen any fingers during the night. He smiled falsely at me.

'Good morning, Mr Morgan. What have you to tell me?' he asked.

I smiled back with the same degree of sincerity. 'I'm not sure. Can I ask some questions first?'

'About what?'

'About the skeleton and about Mason.'

'You can ask all the questions you want, Mr Morgan. Whether or not I answer them is another matter.' I looked at him and then at Fowler. Fowler's nastiness seemed to be rubbing off on his superior.

'First question. You showed me a file that gave details of Tony Capelli's army medical records. From certain data it confirmed the skeleton was his?'

'Correct.'

'Can I see those records again?' I asked. He looked at me and thought about it. Then he looked at Fowler.

'Get the file, Sergeant. Please.' Fowler hesitated just long enough to show that he didn't agree that I should be shown anything. He opened a filing-cabinet drawer and took out a manilla folder, and then closed the cabinet drawer with considerably more violence than was absolutely necessary. He handed it to Peters who opened it, took out the sheets he had shown me before, and placed them reverently in front of me. I looked at them just to be certain I hadn't mis-read them the first time. I hadn't. I slipped my hand into my inside pocket and took out one of the sets of papers Dominic had produced. I laid them alongside Peters's set and stood up and motioned to him. He looked at me, and then stood up and walked round the desk and started to read. After a moment he looked up at me, a faintly puzzled frown on his face.

'Read on,' I told him. 'The interesting bit comes later.' He read the papers in silence. When he had finished he walked back to his chair and sat down again. He nodded at Fowler who pushed himself up out of his seat and stumped across to the desk. When he had finished he looked at me, and for a moment the sneer left his face and he looked genuinely curious. Then habit took over and the sneer came back. He walked back to his chair and sat down again, heavily. I waited until the room stopped vibrating. I picked up the papers I had brought with me and replaced them in my pocket. Peters followed them and his eyes stayed on the slight bulge in my jacket. He reminded me of a dog watching the last place the rabbit was before it disappeared down its hole.

'You said you had questions. You've only asked one,' he said, just to show he had sufficient will-power to overcome his curiosity.

'Just one more. Did you find where Mason was shot?'

'No.'

'Where did you look?' He grinned at me and there was a shade more real humour in the smile that time.

'At the motorway site, the gardens at Bennett's End and the other houses down the same road, the hotel where Mason was staying. Your office and your house and garden.'

'You searched the gardens of all the houses near Bennett's End?'

'Yes, particularly the house next-door, where the plastic sheet came from.'

'What about the third house? Tree Cottage,' I asked. Peters looked at Fowler and received a telepathic message.

'Yes that was searched too.'

'Carefully?'

He looked at me. 'Explain,' he said.

'I think you should look again,' I told him.

'Are you saying you think Mason was killed there?'

'I'm saying it's possible.'

'Why do you think so?'

'You remember the name of the man who gave Alda and Martinelli their alibi?' I asked him. He looked down at the file and flicked over a page.

'Alexander Merrit,' he said.

'Yes,' I said. 'He was renting Tree Cottage.'

I had to admire him. He didn't turn pale or go bright red. He didn't even have hysterics. He simply closed the file and looked at Fowler. The Sergeant went out of the room. He went quietly, too. Peters leaned back in his chair.

'What is going on?' he asked.

'I'm not too sure,' I admitted. 'And before I go any further, I am not going to tell you everything. I'll tell you what I think is relevant for now, and when I turn up anything else that you can use, I'll tell you that too.' I looked at him inquiringly.

'I'm not agreeing to deals before I know what it's all

about,' he said. I grinned at him to show he didn't have a lot of choice.

'If you find evidence that Mason was killed at, or near, the house Merrit was renting, would you say that would reduce the strength of the alibi he gave to Alda and Martinelli?'

'Possibly,' he said carefully.

'Okay,' I said. I reached across and tapped the file on his desk. 'The report you have in there on Tony Capelli. It made a good match with the skeleton?'

'In general respects, yes. As far as the dental information was concerned it was a perfect match.' He pointed at me. 'That report, where did it come from?'

'Originally I expect it came from the same source. Somewhere en route yours got changed. The dental records and the man's height.' I tapped my pocket. 'This one shows that Tony Capelli was five feet five, not five feet eleven, and he had almost perfect teeth. Just two small fillings.'

'How do you know yours isn't the one that got changed?'

'Because I know the route mine followed to get to me.'

'I know the route this one followed.'

'No one on my route had any reason to alter the report,' I told him. He looked at me bleakly.

'You think someone had a reason to alter this one?' he asked.

'It's possible.'

'This one came through the New York Police Department.'

'I know,' I said. He was silent for a moment.

'You know what you're saying?'

'I'm not saying anything, Inspector, I'm just pointing out a possibility.' I reached into my pocket and took out the last report Dominic had obtained for me. I handed it to Peters. 'Look at this man's height and dental record.' He read the parts I indicated. Then he opened the file and compared the dental record to the one he had on Capelli. 'Another perfect match,' I said. He looked at the name on the report.

'Who is Gerald Brown,' he asked.

'A friend of Tony Capelli's.'

'You're saying the skeleton was that of this man, Gerald Brown?'

'Yes.'

'Why are you telling me all this?'

'Because I want someone to know enough of the truth to take things further if it becomes necessary.'

'What does that mean?'

'It means that for the moment I don't want any fuss, Inspector. If Fowler finds anything at Tree Cottage keep it under your hat. Don't say anything to New York, and just stay out of my way until I need you.'

He looked at me coldly. 'I told you I don't make deals,' he said.

'What have you to lose?'

He thought for a moment and then slowly nodded his head. 'Okay, I'll play it your way. For the time being.' I stood up to leave. 'I suppose you know you're setting Kusborski up as the villain of the piece,' he added.

'Am I?'

'He was the one who passed on the doctored report that made the skeleton that of Tony Capelli.'

I grinned at him. 'You're thinking in the right direction. Inspector,' I said. 'Trouble is, you're not thinking far enough.' As I closed the door I looked back and saw him frown. I felt as if I had scored a minor point over him, but all that I had really done was to make sure I wouldn't have the police reopening their inquiries until I had found out the answers to the questions George Capelli had asked. And apart from those questions there were some questions I wanted answering for my own benefit. And one of them was by far the most interesting question of all.

When I reached the office I unlocked the top drawer of the desk and took out the folder I kept there, and replaced the papers I had shown Peters. The slip of paper Dominic had given me listing the names and addresses of the survivors of the crash fell out and, picking it up, I remembered I hadn't reached Genite, and I didn't know where Drucci had moved to. I thought about it for a moment. With all the information Chris Condoli had given me, I didn't think there would be anything either of them could add. I started to push the file back into the drawer. Then I changed my mind and pulled it out again. I placed a call to the number I had obtained for Genite. Ten minutes later the operator called me back and connected me with Victor Genite. Five minutes after that I hung up and sat staring at the telephone. It was just a last-minute change of mind that had made me make the call. If I hadn't changed my mind I wouldn't have made it, and everything might have turned out completely different.

Later I rang Selena Cantrell in New York. I told her what I wanted to know, and she said she would call me back after she had talked to George Capelli. When she rang she asked if it would be safe for her to come to England, and I said I thought it probably would be. She told me the number and time of the flight she intended catching and I said I would meet her at Heathrow.

I stayed in that night. I didn't even go down to the Cyder House. Stanley and I watched a movie on television. It was all about a search for hidden hoards of Nazi gold. It all seemed highly unlikely, and lots of people ended up dead before it finished. Stanley enjoyed it. It left me with an uneasy feeling that I had caught a glimpse of the future.

CHAPTER NINETEEN

She didn't look any less beautiful when I met her off the aircraft, but there was a difference. I couldn't place it at first. Neither of us talked very much as we drove back. I had reserved a room for her at the Talbot in Ripley. I had given her name as Brown; I felt that her own name was too distinctive to risk. I didn't think Peters would be interested in her, not after our last meeting, but I didn't see any point in taking chances. The choice of Brown was my warped sense of humour. After she had registered, and spent a little time in her room freshening up, she came down to where I waited in the hotel's lounge. She looked at me and that was when I identified the difference in her expression. In her eyes there was a look of deep sadness.

'What's happened?' I asked. She looked at me.

'Why do you ask? Should something have happened?'

'You look different. Sad.'

'Are you being the clever detective, Mr Morgan?' she asked with a touch of bitterness. I shook my head.

'No,' I said, 'I'm not. I'm just . . . I'm just expressing concern. That's all.'

She shook her head as if remonstrating with herself. 'I'm sorry, Harry. I'm tired, and as you have guessed there is . . . it's Giorgio. George Capelli. He's very ill. He . . . he has what his father had.' I thought back to the conversation I had had with Kusborski a million years before. If George Capelli had cancer of the throat, then I would soon be minus one client.

'I'm sorry,' I said. I was too, and I have to admit it was largely for mercenary reasons.

'The inquiry continues,' Selena said, almost as if she had been reading my thoughts. 'Even if . . . even if it isn't completed before he . . .' her voice trailed off into silence, and we sat there carefully avoiding looking at one another. After a moment she turned to me again.

'Did you bring the information I asked for?' I said.

'Yes, but first I have to ask why you want to know.'

'Because I have a lot of questions and almost as many answers. The trouble is I don't seem to be able to hang them together.'

'And you think the information you asked for will help?'

'It won't help with most of the questions,' I admitted. 'It may help with one of them. I'm banking on that particular one opening a door to the rest of the answers.' She nodded as if my deliberately vague answer had satisfied her. She opened her bag and took out a piece of paper. It was folded and she left it that way.

'When the old man died,' she began, her eyes shadowing as she touched upon something that came too close to the events that lay ahead for her, 'he left behind only his house and his cars and a few personal possessions. No paintings, no jewellery, no gold, no silver, no money. Nothing, where there should have been millions. Before his death he knew, of course, that he was dying. He called each of his sons to him. Giorgio knows only what he told him, but it is not unreasonable to assume that the old man told the other two the same thing. His fortune was hidden, hidden carefully where no one could find it. Only one man, apart from him, knew where it was. That was a man called Santini, the old man's buffer.' I looked inquiringly at her. 'The buffer is the constant companion of the head of the family,' she went on. 'He goes everywhere, does everything, sees everything. He is more the shadow of the *capo* than his real shadow. Santini hid the fortune for the old man. Then on the old man's instructions three medallions were made, each with a set of figures engraved on the back. Santini will have ensured that the engraver never repeated what the numbers were. The old man gave one medallion to each of his sons. Alone the medallions were useless; together they provided the key to where the fortune was hidden.'

'How?'

'On one medallion there was a five-figure number; on the other two were three-figure numbers. When they were laid together in the right sequence they gave an eleven-figure number.'

'What was the right sequence?'

'Giorgio, Tony, Franco. Tony's had the five-figure number.'

'What does the number mean?'

'It's a map reference.'

'An eleven-figure map reference?'

'Not all of them gave the reference. The first four digits gave the longitudinal reference in reverse. The last four gave the latitudinal reference in the right order. The middle three were meaningless until you stood at the place where the others led you.' I stared at her. After a moment I took a piece of paper and a pencil from my pocket and played with figures.

'The old man must have been a whizz at crossword puzzles and conundrums,' I said.

'He wanted to be sure no one could find his treasure,' she said. I did some more figure juggling.

'There's something I don't understand,' I said. 'All that the three brothers had to do was put the three medallions together and go and collect the loot.'

'No,' she shook her head. 'You didn't know the brothers; their father did. Franco and Giorgio hated each other and they both hated Antonio. They wouldn't have helped one another out of a burning house.'

'Maybe, but if the old man's fortune was big then surely they would have co-operated then, to get a share of millions.'

'That's the point, it would have been a share. Franco and Giorgio would never have settled for a share. Not when they might be able to arrange things so that they got everything.'

'Was that what the old man was trying to do? Set brother against brother?'

'No. He thought they would scheme and feud for a while and then slowly, as the years passed, they would mature, mature to the point where they were capable of running the organisation in place of Fiore Gizzo, and also capable of reconciling themselves and sharing amicably in the fortune their father had left. And then, the old man had reasoned, was when they would need the money.'

'Only it went wrong.'

'Yes,' she said, 'because the old man didn't reckon on Tony going into the army.'

'About that,' I said, 'surely he could have avoided it, with the connections the family must have had?'

'He didn't avoid the draft, because he didn't have to. He volunteered.'

'Did he, now?' I said. 'What kind of a man was Tony?'

'According to Giorgio, Tony was different. He was studious and he preferred reading and listening to music to . . . well, to doing the kind of things his brothers did.'

'Like killing people,' I said unkindly. She looked at me with her sad eyes.

'You have seen too many movies, Harry,' she said. 'The brothers were family, immediate family. Immediate family do not get blood on their hands. That way they can never be touched by the police. No, Tony didn't kill anyone and he never ordered a killing. It is interesting to think what might have happened if he hadn't gone into the army.'

'But he did.'

'Yes. And he came here to England and ... died?' Her voice ended on a questioning note. I shook my head.

'I don't know,' I said. 'The skeleton was that of a man named Gerald Brown, a friend of Tony's. All the evidence points to Tony being in the aircraft when it crashed. He wasn't one of the five known survivors.'

'Could he have survived without anyone knowing?'

'It's possible. Anything is possible, I suppose, but if he did survive he had to find somewhere to hide, somewhere he could hide for a long time.' She looked at me curiously.

'Have you found anything to make you think he did?' she asked.

'Not exactly. Tony had a girl friend here, an English girl called Mary Graham. She was around until just after the war ended, then she disappeared, but not before telling a relative that she was getting married and emigrating to Canada. She didn't get married, at least not in England, and she didn't go to Canada. I checked.'

'You think maybe she and Tony ...?'

'I can't think of any reason for her going off without telling anyone. And laying a false trail into the bargain.'

'But where?'

'Where the numbers on his medallion told them to go,' I said.

'But no single medallion was enough to tell them that. Do you mean he had found the number on Giorgio's and Franco's medallion?'

'No. With only his own number he could narrow the field. The old man wasn't as clever as he thought. Either that or he was being too clever. Maybe he wanted Tony to have his fortune, and didn't want the older sons to know he'd given it to Tony.'

'I still don't see what you're ... how can ...? She shook her head in bewilderment.

'Did you bring Giorgio's medallion?' I asked.

'No.'

'But you brought the number?'

'Yes.'

'What is it?' She unfolded the piece of paper she held and handed it to me. I looked at it.

'That narrows it down a lot,' I said.

'How?' she asked.

I grinned at her. 'It's a secret,' I said.

I went out of the hotel, climbed into the Volvo, and drove down to the public library in Guildford. I found a copy of the *Times Atlas* in the reference department and spent an hour with it. I made notes of everything that seemed relevant, and then handed the book back and went to the office. Nothing seemed to have changed. The world still wasn't beating a path to my door. I rang Tommy Andrews and told him I needed Stanley for a few days and he got all upset. I told him that my need was greater than his, and after a slightly edgy exchange we hung up. Then I rang the police station and asked for Peters.

'Busy?' I asked.

'Yes.'

'Anything that might interest me?'

'The garden at Tree Cottage,' he said.

'What have you found?'

'Blood and a bullet.'

'What kind of bullet?'

'.44 magnum, possibly fired from a Smith & Wesson, but that part's a guess at the moment. Mean anything?'

'No, not yet. Will you do something for me?'

'What?'

'Call the NYPD and tell them you know that the report proving that the skeleton was Capelli's was phoney. And tell them it was me that told you.'

'What are you after? Thinking of applying for a job?'

'It's called starting a hare,' I said, and hung up before he had time to ask me silly questions to which I either couldn't or wouldn't be able to find answers.

Before going home I called British Airways and asked for the earliest booking they could give me. They were battling with a baggage-handler's strike and there was a thirty-six hour delay. I couldn't see that the delay would matter and I booked three seats.

I felt quite cheerful driving home. As far as I could see I had covered all the angles. It took me over an hour of searching before I found the folder where I kept our passports. They were still valid but only just. Neither had been used. I had got them when I was planning on taking Stanley on holiday, but we hadn't gone. That had been the time he had come home and found me alone with a woman. Some of the cheerfulness evaporated.

CHAPTER TWENTY

I unfastened my seat-belt and tried unsuccessfully to pop my ears. I reached over and unfastened Stanley's seat-belt. He didn't seem to notice; he was glued to the tiny porthole that was a 707's way of showing we weren't really thought of as sardines in a can. The stewardesses had looked slightly alarmed at Stanley's size, and had suggested that he would be best put in an aisle seat where he could spread out a little. I said I would prefer that he had a window seat to keep him occupied, and by then the girls had noticed that Stanley's permanent smile wasn't quite what it had seemed to be at first. He sat there, his knees almost as high as his chin, totally engrossed in what was, without doubt, the most exciting experience of his life. I'm not sure, even now, of my motives in taking him. There always had been an element of danger in what faced us, and with the way I'd chosen to play things the degree of risk had increased. But he was a person I could trust – in fact, the only person available to me that I could trust. That, I had reasoned to myself, might prove to be more important than the obvious drawbacks of his presence.

I was in the centre of the three seats on our side of the aisle, and with Stanley fully occupied I turned to Selena. She had accepted my sudden instruction to pack and leave the hotel, and with only a few minutes' delay she had been ready to leave. I took care not to give her an opportunity to use a telephone at either the hotel or the airport, particularly after she knew what the flight destination was. It wasn't that I didn't trust her; it just made things less complicated.

'I'm sorry I've kept you in the dark,' I said.

'I expect you had your reasons.'

'I think so.'

'Why Sardinia?' she asked.

'It's the most likely of the possible places.'

'Are you planning on explaining or are you just going to sit there looking smug?' she asked. I grinned at her, and after a moment she smiled back.

'Okay,' I said. I took a piece of paper from my pocket and a pen and scribbled some numbers. 'Say those were the eleven numbers. The middle five were on Tony's medallion. Right?'

She nodded. 'Yes, but . . .'

'Wait,' I said. 'The three middle digits meant nothing for the moment. But the two outer digits gave Tony a starting point. They were the first numbers of the longitude and latitude of where the old man's money was hidden.'

'Yes, but . . .' she said again.

'Wait. Now the old man didn't say whether the longitude was east or west, and he didn't say whether the latitude was north or south, so there could be four possible locations on the globe. The opening digit of the references that were on Tony's medallion would let him reduce those four possible locations to fairly restricted areas. Not too restricted, but at least he would know which parts of the haystack he should be looking in. The chances were, with water covering so much of the globe, that one or more of the locations would be in an ocean, and that would limit his areas of search still further. After that he simply needed intelligence and time.' I had been accompanying my explanations with little sketches and Selena nodded.

'Yes,' she said. 'I see how that would help Tony, but how

is it going to help us? All we have is the number on Giorgio's medallion.'

'That's all you have,' I said. 'I have the number that was on Tony's medallion.' I looked at her. Her eyes were a little brighter and I thought it seemed to be genuine interest and not just cupidity.

'How? Have you found the medallion?'

'No. I traced the names of the five men who were known to have survived the crash. One was killed later in the war, one I can't find, but I talked to the other three. One told me nothing. One told me a lot, it was through him that I found that the skeleton was that of Gerry Brown. He also told me about Mary Graham. The third one didn't seem to know very much at all. Until I asked him if he had ever seen Tony with a medallion. He said he had. Once when he and Tony were alone in the barracks. It had fallen from Tony's wallet and this other man, Victor Genite, picked it up and handed it back to Tony.'

'Well?'

'As he did so he glanced at it. He said it felt uneven underneath. That would be the rose design. The face he looked at was smooth and it had a number engraved on it.'

'You can't mean he remembered it. Not after thirty years.'

'Yes he did and for a very good reason.'

'What?'

'There are some things a man never forgets. One thing is supposed to be his service number. I wouldn't know myself but I've heard enough men say it to accept that it's true.'

'But . . .'

'The five numbers on the coin were the same as the last five numbers of Victor Genite's service number. He had no difficulty in remembering it. No difficulty at all.' I picked up the paper and pen again. I wrote down the five-figure number and showed it to her. She looked at it and nodded her head. 'As I said before,' I went on, 'there are, theoretically, four places on the globe that could start with the combination of the opening digits Tony had. Two of the four are in the middle of the South Atlantic Ocean. The other two also include a lot of water, but enough interesting bits of land to have given Tony room for thought!'

'What land?'

I opened the map I had brought with me. 'This is a small-scale map of the world, but it's best for this. Tony's number was 01283. That meant that the longitude reference began with zero and the latitude reference began with the three. If the reference was arranged west-north, then the area includes a part of the North Atlantic with a little of the Mediterranean. The land in that area includes part of Algeria, most of Morocco and a tiny bit of Portugal. If the reference was arranged east-north the area covered is a larger part of the Mediterranean plus part of Algeria again, most of Tunisia, the Balearic Islands and about half of Sardinia.' I looked at Selena. 'George Capelli's number was 309,' I said. 'If we reverse that and add the zero from Tony's number to the front of it we have 0903. That's the longitude, and the latitude is anywhere between thirty degrees and thirty-nine degrees fifty-nine minutes.' I reached into my pocket and pulled out the notes I had made from the atlas. 'You asked me why Sardinia. Well, I have to admit that I liked the thought of Portugal and Morocco because both Lisbon and Casablanca were in the area, and both seemed the kind of place a man wanting to hide illegally earned money and valuables would have gone. At least, then, in the 'thirties. But then I thought a little more, and I came to the conclusion that Joe Capelli was probably a simple man at heart.' I looked at her carefully. 'I'm not saying that in the sense of a nice little old man. He was an evil man, as evil as Capone and Torrio and Luciano and all the rest of them, but he was also very much a man with his roots firmly in the old ways.'

'How do you know what he was like?' she asked.

'I read a book.'

'Books are what is in the mind of the writer.'

'Maybe. Anyway I reckoned that Joe was probably a man who had roots.'

'But his roots were in Naples. That doesn't explain why we are going to Sardinia.'

'Because he was Italian, and the guy who hid the loot – Santini you called him – he was Italian. Sardinia is the only place among those I've named where Italian is spoken. Santini would want to operate where he wouldn't stand out as a total stranger.'

'So you think the money is on the island?'

'It's possible.'

She pointed her finger at the map. 'It's a big island.'

'Yes,' I agreed, 'but the northern half is above the fortieth parallel. That just leaves the southern half.'

'It's still big.'

'You're forgetting. We know it is hidden along the longitude nine degrees three minutes.'

'But still . . .'

'And then there are the remaining three numbers on Tony's medallion.'

'One, two, eight.'

'Yes. Don't forget that was all Tony had.'

'I suppose you know what that means?'

'I think so,' I said. I showed her the notes I had made. 'After you had given me the number on George Capelli's medallion I looked at an atlas. There are four towns, villages I suppose would be a better word, on that longitude. Laconi, Nuragus, Guasila and Monastir. For good measure I wrote down some that were close; Meana is about two minutes off to the east and Samatzai about one minute off to the west. All of them are close to the road that runs between Cagliari and Nuoro. Only two of them are actually on that road.'

'So?'

'So the road is the SS 128.'

She was silent for a moment. 'Then if Tony did reason it out the way you have, even without his brothers' numbers he might still have concluded that the fortune was hidden somewhere along the SS 128.'

'Yes.'

'It's a long road.'

'He's had a long time to look.'

'If he's still alive.'

'If he's still alive.'

'How are you so sure he reasoned it the way you have done?'

'Because while I can accept that he might have volunteered for the army to get away from his brothers, I can't see any reason for him volunteering to join a special unit. Except that the ultimate destination of that unit was to be the invasion of Italy.'

'Italy isn't Sardinia.'

'No, and Tony Capelli wasn't a general. It would have been a reasonably intelligent guess that the invasion would take place that way. It didn't. Instead they went in through Pantellaria and Sicily. Half-way through August 1943, Sicily fell, and the invasion of the mainland took place on 3rd September. That was where the Dakota was headed. The special unit was to go in ahead of the troops. But they didn't because they crashed. By then Tony probably knew he wasn't going to Sardinia anyway, so if he did survive the plane crash he had nothing to lose by going into hiding and letting everyone believe he was dead.'

'But why did someone try to make it appear that the skeleton was Tony's?'

'A good question. Maybe we'll find the answer when we reach Sardinia.'

'How?'

'That depends on who else is there. Or rather who else arrives after we do.'

'Who knows we are on our way to Sardinia? You took care that I didn't tell anyone.'

'I know, but I did arrange for a hint to be dropped, and it will be interesting to see if anyone reacts to it.'

'Will they, whoever they are, be able to find what we're looking for?'

'I expect so.'

'How?'

'If word reaches Frank Capelli it won't take him long to find out that we are heading for Sardinia. He will assume that it is because we think the old man hid his fortune there.'

'So?'

'So Frank has the last three digits of the latitude. If it is on Sardinia the missing first digit has to be three. That gives him a clear line across the island. He doesn't know about the road number, but there can't be that many towns and villages on that particular latitude.' As I spoke I felt uneasy. Our thirty-six-hour delay in getting off the ground could have given a fast-moving operation time to get in front of us.

'You didn't tell me because you wanted to see whether I could be trusted or not?' Selena accused.

'Yes. It also made life easier. With George out of the running because you haven't told him anything, that left Frank Capelli and his friends and maybe, maybe someone else.'

'Who?'

'It's a secret.'

'You said that once before. It's irritating.'

'I expect it is.'

She leaned forward and looked across at Stanley. When she spoke again her voice was lower. 'Why did you bring Stanley?'

'I'm not certain. I felt it would be nice to have a friend I knew I could trust. If you'll forgive the slight.'

'But he could be in danger. You haven't told me anything about him but it's obvious . . .' She hesitated. 'Forgive me but it is obvious that he will be out of his depth if there is trouble.'

'Yes,' I said. I felt uneasy. She was simply repeating the doubts I had already felt about my motives for bringing Stanley.

'Before, you seemed concerned that he didn't find us alone,' she went on. 'Now he's travelling with us. What has changed?'

'I think he likes you,' I said. She looked at me.

'What about you, do you like me?' she asked.

'I thought that would be obvious,' I said. We looked at each other and after a moment she turned away. I think her colour heightened a little, but maybe that was just wishful thinking.

Of the three of us only Stanley seemed sorry when the flight ended. I think he could have gone on for ever.

Before we left Elmas airport at Cagliari I hired a car. It was a Fiat; there wasn't much choice. I let Stanley drive because that gave me the opportunity to keep my eyes open in case we were being observed. If we were, I didn't see anyone. I had picked up a guide book at the airport, and I directed Stanley to the AGIP Motel at Pirri where I booked us into two rooms. When the manager realised that Stanley and I were sharing and Selena was alone, he favoured me with the kind of look only an Italian could have given an Englishman in those circumstances. I ignored him. I gave Selena half an hour to wash and change, and I spent the time hovering near the switchboard in the reception area. I didn't think she would try to call anyone, but I didn't want to take the chance. If the hint I had asked Peters to drop in New York had had the effect I hoped for, then I would have enough on my plate as it was.

CHAPTER TWENTY-ONE

The two villages that lay on the correct longitude were Nuragus and Laconi, and we looked at Nuragus first. We spent a day there, and there was nothing to give any hint that we were any closer to what we were looking for than we had been before we left England. Our search was not helped by the fact that none of us knew what it was we *were* looking for. Stanley, of course, didn't know we were looking for anything at all.

We spent a slightly depressed evening watching Stanley eat his way through a restaurant's entire menu. After a cautious start, and after I had convinced him that scrambled eggs, blackcurrant jam, and fish and chips were not forthcoming, he experimented and then went wild. He started with tunny-fish roe, went on to Sardinian sausage before the waiter could hide the hors d'oeuvres tray, and then sank three bowls of *zimino*. By the time Selena and I had moved on to our main course, trout and asparagus for her and sea bream for me, the restaurant staff had begun to realise they had a challenge on their hands. With two waiters actually serving, and others hovering in the background in case they were needed, Stanley began the grand attack. He demolished a lobster that had probably been towed back by the fishing boat that caught it; it was too big to have been carried on board. Then he asked for a repeat and much to my astonishment the chef produced a twin brother to the first one. Then he waded into spit-roasted kid, and finished off with a mountain of cheese, and several complicated-looking sweet dishes made largely of almonds. I felt limp afterwards, and I tried to persuade him to take a large dose of indigestion mixture. He declined.

'I don't need that, Harry. That was nice. I enjoyed it. Why haven't we been here before, Harry?' I looked at him as if I was seeing him for the first time.

'It never seemed possible, Stanley,' I said.

'I like it here, Harry,' he said simply and beamed at me, and at Selena, and at the waiters, and the chef who had emerged from his kitchen to inspect the man who had very nearly emptied his stock cupboard. I smiled at him.

'I'm glad, Stanley,' I said. 'Maybe we'll be able to come back again one day.'

I drove the Fiat back to the motel, and by the time we reached Pirri, Stanley seemed about ready for bed. I left Selena in the car and settled Stanley in our room. Then I parked the car and walked with her across to her room. I saw the manager watching us and he seemed to be regarding me with a little more respect.

'Can I come in, just for a few minutes?' I asked. She nodded and opened the door. I followed her in. She sat in the only armchair and, after looking at a hard cane-backed chair, I sat on the edge of the bed.

'He's so . . . gentle,' she said.

'Stanley? Yes he is – most of the time.' She looked at me inquiringly.

'What are you frightened of? You said you would tell me when you knew me better. Do you know me better now?'

I looked at her. 'You seemed to think there was some doubt that I ever would,' I said.

'I suppose you must know me better than most people,' she said. I thought about her answer. As far as I could see I hardly knew her at all.

'How did you meet George Capelli?' I asked. She turned away, her eyes darkening.

'I was a secretary with a law firm. He was a client.'

'Mason?'

'Yes, John was the man I worked for – then.'

'What happened?'

'George came to John after his wife died. We knew who he was, of course, and at first John wanted nothing to do with him, but he made it clear that he wanted John to deal with purely personal matters. Nothing to do with the business.'

'His clean lawyer,' I said. She nodded her head slowly.

'I suppose you could say that,' she agreed. 'Then one day he came to the office when John wasn't there, and we talked and he invited me out to lunch, and we talked some more and after that he began to call me – every day. He was . . . is a very charming man, and it was easy to forget the kind of things his name was linked to. Eventually he asked me to leave John and to go and work for him as his secretary, and live in at his house. I agreed. I knew where it would lead, of course, and I didn't mind in the least.' She looked at me as if challenging me to argue.

'You live together?' I asked.

'Yes. Does it shock you?'

'Why should it?'

'An age gap of almost forty years; a daughter of an East-Coast aristocrat and a son of old Joe Capelli. It shocked a lot of people.' There was a note of mingled bitterness and sadness in her voice.

'Your family.'

She nodded. 'Yes. They disowned me. Now Giorgio is the only family I have and now he is . . . now he is dying.' Her eyes seemed unnaturally bright.

'I'm sorry,' I said.

'I wasn't asking for sympathy.'

'I didn't mean it that way,' I said. 'I meant I am sorry that I pried.'

She smiled suddenly. 'I expect you were avoiding answering my questions. I was the one doing the prying.'

'You mean about Stanley? Ah well, we all have our . . . we all have problems.'

'You were going to say we all have our crosses to bear.'

'Maybe I was. If I was, I'm sorry for being cynical and self-indulgent.'

'Why do you look after him?'

'Someone has to, and I seem to be the only one who can control him when . . . when something goes wrong.'

'Tell me,' she said. I told her. I told her about Stanley and the fight when we were children at school, and how he had nearly killed Tommy Andrews, and I told her about the fight in the street at Walsall when he had almost killed the last of the gang that had tried to beat me up. Then I stopped.

'What about the time you were with a woman?' she asked. I remembered.

It had happened when we had been living in Yorkshire. It was just after we had joined Tommy, and we were working on the site of the M1 extension into Leeds. I had been going through a period of enforced celibacy. Enforced unless you have no taste at all, that is. There are always a few women to pick up if you get really desperate, but where we were working was out of the way, and the local talent left a great deal to be desired. Then Tommy had hired a new secretary, and instead of the usual be-wellingtoned refugee from the chorus of *Götterdämmerung*, he had shown real taste for the first and, as it turned out, last time. She was small and dark and very pretty, and the men on the site had gone after her like hounds after a fox. But, like a fox, she had evaded them neatly and carefully without offending any one of them.

Then, when she had convinced everybody that she was untouchable, she had offered herself to me so openly and unreservedly that it had taken me some time to realise that it was really happening. Once I had recovered, I didn't let my good fortune go to waste. I was with her every night, and occasionally during the day when circumstances permitted. Week-ends were long, glorious, sexual romps. She told me she loved me and I believed her, and I told her that I loved her and she believed me. I never thought about Stanley, and although I took no steps to hide from him what was happening he had never seen us together, other than when I drove her home from the site. Most of our time together was spent in the flat she rented in the nearest small town. Then one day, for some reason I can no longer remember, we didn't go to her flat. We went instead to the caravan that Stanley and I shared. I have said before that Stanley could, and usually did, move silently, and neither of us heard a sound. I suppose what we were doing made hearing difficult anyway. The first thing I knew was when someone grabbed hold of me and threw me at the wall of the caravan. I picked myself up and he was standing there, the tiny, dark-haired girl in his hands, looking for all the world like a giant wooden carving. Nothing moved except his arms as he shook her, backwards and forwards, his face set and all traces of his familiar smile wiped completely from it. The girl's head was snapping to and fro, and even as it was happening I remember thinking clearly that if I didn't stop him her neck would break. I tried to stop him. I attacked him with my bare hands and I hit him with everything I could find, but there is very little in a caravan that is big enough or heavy enough to stop a man like Stanley. I ran outside, completely naked, and under the caravan I found a length of steel tube we used as a rigid tow-bar. When I went back inside the caravan, Stanley was still shaking the girl, only by then she was silent. I remember thinking, my God he's killed her, and then I hit him with the tube. I had to hit him three times before he dropped her.

After I had told her the story, Selena sat quietly for a moment.

'What happened?' she said eventually.

'The girl came round. It seemed like a miracle. She wasn't really hurt at all, very bad bruising on her arms where he had held her but that was all the physical damage there was. She sat there, staring at him. He wasn't unconscious, although I'd hit him hard enough. He didn't look at her once. She was terrified of him, naturally enough. I talked to her, kept talking to her, then gradually she began to cry and talk at the same time. I think she had been afraid at first that he was attacking her to, well, she thought he was going to rape her. When she realised that it hadn't been that kind of attack she calmed down a little.'

'Were the police called?'

'No. It took a great deal of talking to convince her that it wouldn't do anyone any good if they were. I helped her to dress, then I dressed, and I took her back to her flat in the car. She wouldn't let me in. She said she would see me the next day at the site. So I drove away and left her there. I never saw her again.' We were both silent, both with our own thoughts.

'Have you had a permanent relationship since then?' Selena asked, eventually.

'Not really.' I thought about Julie but that no longer seemed to qualify. 'There have been occasions when I've got close – celibacy isn't my strong suit – but every time I felt like making things more permanent I remembered the girl – and Stanley trying to kill her.'

'So you're a permanent bachelor?' she said. I looked at her carefully.

'Are you asking if I'm too old to change?' I said. She

looked at me, and her skin darkened slightly as she recognised the clumsy trap I was trying to lay.

'Does anyone else know what happened?' she asked, changing the subject.

'No.'

'Do you want an amateur psychiatrist's opinion?' she asked after some moments had passed.

'I'll tell you when I've heard it,' I said, smiling.

'Those were the only three occasions when Stanley ... snapped?'

'Yes.'

'The first two were when he thought you were being attacked. The third was when he thought he was being attacked.'

'Attacked? How?'

'The girl was taking you away from him. Additionally he must have had some idea what sex was about, even allowing for his condition. What he saw was very possibly a severe shock to him. Mutual oral sex is a little advanced for someone with a mental age like his.'

I nodded. 'Maybe,' I said. 'Maybe you're right.'

'And if I am?'

'If you are, I'm still left looking after Stanley.'

'With you not there, the cause of his three violent outbursts would have been absent,' she said.

I shook my head. 'Too facile, Selena. No, don't be angry,' I said as she made a sound of exasperation. 'You can't build a case out of three widely separate events you've heard second-hand from one of the participants.'

'You could try it for a while,' she said.

'Perhaps,' I said again.

'There is another way of looking at it,' she said quietly.

'What?'

'That you need him.'

'Need him?'

'Some people have crosses to bear because they need to have them.' I shook my head and stood up.

'Now you're getting too devious for me,' I said.

'Too devious or too near the truth?' she asked. I didn't answer and after a moment she turned away. 'Ask yourself another question, Harry,' she said, her voice slightly muffled. 'Ask yourself why you've brought him here.' I walked to the door and opened it. The night was bright and pleasantly cool after the heat of the day.

'I'll see you in the morning,' I said and closed the door. I walked back to my room and went in. Stanley was asleep, his huge body stretched out awkwardly on the normal-sized double bed. I undressed and swilled my face in the tepid water that came from the cold tap. I pulled a chair up close to the bed and sat down, swinging my legs up on to the bed. Stanley stirred in his sleep but did not waken. I closed my eyes and tried not to think of the questions Selena had asked. I wasn't very successful, and I didn't sleep much. I was pleased when it was morning, and I had something to do that prevented me from thinking too much.

CHAPTER TWENTY-TWO

Breakfast was frugal because neither Selena nor I seemed to have much of an appetite, and because Stanley's refusal to take anything for potential indigestion proved to have been an error on his part. None of us spoke much as we drove out of Cagliari and turned off the main road on to the SS 128 just after we had passed through Monastir. I was driving and Stanley was next to me, with the front passenger-seat pushed as far back as its mechanism allowed. Selena sat in the back, and for the first time since we had reached the island she was wearing sunglasses. Perhaps she needed the shelter they afforded.

Laconi isn't a very big place and it didn't take us long to discover, as we had at Nuragus the previous day, that there was nothing immediately apparent that we could connect with the Capelli family. We found a small bar in a shady side street, and we went inside to rest and think about what to do next. We were the only people there, apart from the proprietor, until a small, white-haired old man came in and ordered a drink. They chattered away furiously and the words washed over me in a meaningless wave. I sensed Selena stiffen and, looking at her, I saw that she was watching the two men, her head slightly tilted. I waited until the little old man had left before I spoke.

'What was it? What were they saying?' I asked. She looked at me, and there was that smallest of hesitations people make when they are debating with themselves whether or not to speak the truth.

'My Italian isn't very good. I managed a few words because Giorgio likes to speak it when we ... when we are alone.' I nodded impatiently. 'They were speaking in dialect,' she went on, 'but I think I heard the old man use the words ... he said something about Rosa Medaglione.'

'What does that ...?' I stopped and answered my own question. 'Rose Medallion.' She nodded, her face tense with excitement.

'Yes,' she said.

'Ask him.' I pointed at the proprietor who was reading a newspaper. She went over to him and I heard them conversing slowly, and after a moment I stopped straining to hear the words which I would not have understood anyway. After several minutes she came back and sat down again at the table.

'Well?' I said.

'I don't know if it's what we are looking for.'

'What?' I asked impatiently.

'A short way outside the town there is a small factory, a bottling plant. They bottle wine for one of the biggest vineyards in the area. Their main product is a *Moscato*. It's sold under a trade name ... Rosa Medaglione.' I looked at her, and then at the proprietor, as if seeking his confirmation that it was true. I shook my head slowly.

'It seems ...' I stopped and kept my thoughts to myself. I stood up. 'We'd better go and have a look,' I said.

The bottling plant was a stone-built, two-storey structure. The only exceptional thing about the place was the silence. There wasn't a sound, not a clink of a bottle, nothing. I glanced at my watch. It was still well short of midday and, as far as I was aware, it wasn't a public holiday. I told Stanley to climb into the driving seat, and told him to take Selena back to the hotel if there was any trouble. He looked at me oddly.

'What kind of trouble, Harry?'

'Any kind,' I said.

'I don't think you should go in there alone,' Selena said.

'And I think you should stay here and keep quiet,' I said. Before either of them said anything more I walked quickly across the hard-packed earth of the courtyard in front of the building and tried a white-painted door. It opened and I went in. Inside, the building was cool and dark and it took a moment for my eyes to adjust. Standing about five yards from the door, looking at me with round, dark eyes, were two young women and five men. Their eyes held a mixture of fear and bewilderment. I heard a sound behind me and I turned round. The door was swinging shut and behind it stood Nicola Martinelli. He held a gun in his left hand, held it with a negligent authority that removed from my mind any ideas about trying to take it from him almost before they were born. He gestured to his right.

'Go up the stairs, Morgan, and move slowly.' I looked where he was pointing and moved towards the flight of stone steps that led up to the first floor. When I was half-way up I heard the door below me open. I glanced back and saw Martinelli was looking out. I heard him mutter a curse, and at the same instant I heard the Fiat take off with a roar as the wheels spun on the dry earth. Selena must have seen Martinelli and recognised him – Stanley would not have moved that fast without prompting. Above me another door opened and Martinelli's partner, Mario Alda, stood there waiting for me. I watched the gun in his hand carefully. He seemed slightly less casual with it than his partner. I reckoned that, although Martinelli seemed the most dangerous, Alda would be the one to watch. I don't like people who are unpredictable.

The room was an office of sorts. Around the walls were advertisements for the products, and there was a clean clutter of papers and files and cardboard and packing and string. In the centre of the room was a table, large and heavy; it had probably taken several big strong men to get it up there. Seated at the table were three people, two men and a woman. If I'd met them separately, or even together in another place, I doubt if I would have recognised them. After all, the only pictures I had seen of them were many years old. One of the men was dressed in a black suit that looked like vicuna with a white-on-white shirt and a black tie with a discreet pattern of small white flecks. He had a white silk handkerchief in the outside breast pocket of his jacket. I couldn't see his feet but I took a bet he was wearing black silk socks and black hand-made shoes. Altogether he was wearing the equivalent of what I had paid for my estate car. His head was large and his tightly-curled black hair showed no signs of grey although he was almost sixty. His face was heavily jowled, and he had a straight line where most people have lips. His eyes looked like flat black pebbles. He was Frank Capelli. The other man and the woman were sitting close together, the woman's hand tight in the man's as if seeking protection he seemed unlikely to be able to give. Plump, with a round face that was probably normally permanently smiling, she still had a prettiness the advancing years had not faded. Her hair was a mixture of blond and grey. I doubt that I would ever have recognised her as Mary Graham, certainly not from the blurred snapshot she had sent to Mrs Kenny, her old relative in Oxford. The man whose hand she held was stocky, and the arms that thrust aggressively from the tightly-rolled sleeves of the grey woollen shirt he wore were heavily muscular. Like Frank Capelli, his hair showed no signs of grey. His face was strong, and there was a deep cleft in his chin below a mouth that looked as if it normally smiled a lot. It wasn't smiling now. Nobody introduced us, but I knew I had finally discovered that Tony Capelli hadn't died in the plane crash.

The man in the black suit looked questioningly at Alda.

'This is Morgan. The one with the dummy cousin,' Alda said.

'Ah. So you're the one. Sit down, Mr Morgan.' Frank Capelli's voice was thin and reedy, quite unlike the hoarse rasp of his brother George, but then he didn't have George's problem. I sat down. He waved his hand at the man and woman. 'Meet my brother, Tony Capelli.' I nodded at the man in the grey shirt. He looked at me impassively. After all, he didn't know whose side I was on. 'And his wife Maria,' Frank Capelli was saying. I looked at her.

'I wouldn't have recognized you from the photograph,' I said, 'the one you gave to Mrs Kenny.' She looked startled, and then something like a smile touched her face for a moment.

'Is she still alive?'

'Yes, just.' I became aware that Frank Capelli was looking at me curiously.

'You're English?' he asked the woman. She nodded her head. He looked at me. 'You knew?'

'Obviously,' I said.

'Well, maybe you're not as dumb as I was told.' He looked at Alda. 'You didn't tell me she was English,' he said softly.

'I . . . we didn't know,' Alda said anxiously as Martinelli came into the room.

'What didn't we know?' Martinelli asked.

'That Tony's wife is English. I thought you were supposed to find out everything,' Capelli said. Martinelli looked at him without emotion.

'Does it matter?' he asked. He gave the clear impression that whatever Frank Capelli was, he would not take from him any criticism he thought unjustified. Frank Capelli must have thought the same, because he abruptly turned away and changed the subject.

'I heard a car,' he said. 'Who was it?'

'Morgan's cousin, the big dummy, he was driving. There was a woman in the back. I didn't see her clearly, but I guess it would be Cantrell.'

Capelli nodded. 'So they're out of the way. They won't go to the police, Selena won't risk involving Giorgio.' He looked at his brother. 'Selena's Giorgio's lady friend.' Abruptly his manner changed. 'Okay, let's move faster. Where is it hidden?'

Tony Capelli looked at him calmly. 'There is nothing to hide, Franco,' he answered. 'It is all gone.'

'Crap. This dump didn't cost you the millions the old man left.'

'You are mistaken. Our father did not leave millions. There was only sufficient to buy this place and the vineyard in the valley.'

'Now listen to me, Tony . . .'

'No, Franco, I am telling you the truth. I expected there would be more, but there wasn't. Perhaps it was Santini. Perhaps he took it elsewhere. Hid it for himself.'

'Santini? You don't expect me to buy that. Santini was the old man's buffer. He would not have touched anything that belonged to the *capo*.'

'How can you be sure? And how else can you account for the fact that there was nothing here.'

'I don't have to account for it, because I don't believe it,' Franco said. He motioned to Alda who pushed his gun into a shoulder holster, and stepped behind the woman, and pulled her up and away from the table. Tony Capelli started to rise and Martinelli stepped forward and gestured with his gun. Capelli sank back into his chair. Alda wound his fingers into the woman's hair and a short-bladed knife materialised in his free hand and pressed into her neck.

'Now, Tony. Tell me again.' Frank Capelli said.

'I have told you, I . . .' There was an almost imperceptible nod from his brother and Alda's hand moved. Maria Capelli screamed thinly, and a tiny drop of blood appeared where the knife rested against her throat.

'Next time, Tony, next time will be the last time.'

The younger of the Capelli brothers slumped forward, resting his head against his hands. 'Very well, I will tell you.' He looked up. 'Let her go.' Nobody moved. 'Let her go,' he said savagely. The elder Capelli looked at Alda and nodded. Alda released the woman and stepped back, the knife disappearing and being replaced by his gun with almost no discernible movement. The woman sat down heavily and her husband reached out and put his arm around her. He let his lips brush against her cheek and then turned to his brother.

'You are right, it was here. I used a little for the purchase of the business and then I decided that I wanted no more.'

'Then why did you keep it hidden? You could have told me, us, your brothers.'

'I was dead as far as you were concerned. I wanted to stay that way. And I did not want the money to be used for ... for the purposes to which you would have put it.'

His brother laughed, a tinny sound that held no humour. 'A conscience. Is that what you have?'

'Perhaps. I do not think you would understand, Franco.'

'Perhaps I understand more than you think, my brother. 'Okay, enough talk. Tell me where it is hidden.'

'I will have to take you. It is in the north of the island and it is very difficult to find. Even Neptune's treasure is not as well hidden.' I didn't miss the flicker that came and went in his wife's eyes. I glanced carefully at the other three men in the room and, as far as I could see, none of them had noticed.

'Very well,' Frank Capelli stood up. 'We will go, you and I and ... you,' he said, pointing at Martinelli. 'And you,' he nodded at Alda, 'stay here with the woman. If he is telling lies I will telephone you here. You will kill her.'

'What about him?' Martinelli pointed at me.

'He is working for Giorgio. He no longer interests me,' Frank said.

'No I'm not,' I said. He looked at me, waiting. 'Your brother hired me to find out if Tony was alive or dead, that's all. Now I know, I'm no longer working for him.'

'You are lying. My brother wants the money just as I do.'

'What does he want money for? Where he's going he'll have no use for it.'

'What do you mean?' he asked. I looked at him; he seemed genuinely puzzled.

'He's dying,' I said. 'Cancer of the throat.' For the first time an expression appeared in his flat black eyes, and it wasn't one of sadness.

'So. That is the second time you have told me something I did not know. You are a surprising man, Mr Morgan. What do you want?'

I thought fast. 'A job. You can use a man in England. You people are still thin on the ground over there.'

He thought about it for a moment. 'There is no time to decide now. I will decide later. In the meantime you stay here.' He looked at Alda. 'If he gives you trouble, kill him too.' He walked swiftly to the door and went down the stairs. Martinelli gestured at Tony and he stood, touched his wife's cheek and followed. A few minutes later I heard a car engine start up at the rear of the building, and then the engine became louder as the car drove around to the front. Then it faded as they drove away.

No one spoke for several minutes. There was silence in the building below, and I wondered what Martinelli had done with the employees I had seen when I had first walked in. Maria Capelli sat quietly, her face taut with stress.

'What happened after the crash?' I asked her. I wanted to know, and it occurred to me that if I was to do anything about Alda and his gun I had to put him off his guard. She made herself answer me.

'Tony was thrown clear. He was shaken but not badly hurt. He realised no one had seen him, and when the aircraft exploded he knew that if he could get away he would be able to disappear and perhaps start a new life. He succeeded.'

'What happened to Gerry Brown?' I asked.

'Who?'

'Gerry Brown. He was Tony's friend.'

'Oh yes, I remember him. I met him with Tony.' She shook her head. 'He must have died in the crash. He wasn't one of the survivors. At first, I didn't think Tony had survived. I went to see the five who did. Then a few days later Tony turned up at the house where I was living.'

Suddenly I heard a sound from below. Nothing I could identify and Alda heard it too. He went to the door and looked down. Then he came back in to the room.

'Where are the workmen and the women?' Maria Capelli asked.

'They're in the stock-room. They can't get out so don't get any ideas they're going to rescue you,' Alda said. We sat in silence, and then I heard the sound again. This time Alda ignored it, but I was certain that it was closer and unmuffled; not the kind of sound made by someone in a locked room.

'How did you keep him hidden?' I asked the woman hurriedly. She looked puzzled. 'Tony,' I said, 'how did you hide him from the authorities?'

'It wasn't too hard. You see no one was looking for him. They thought he was dead. I kept him hidden for a few weeks until we were certain it was safe, and I kept my job at the camp. Then, later, I took another job farther out in the country where no one knew me. He still had to hide most of the time, but things were not too bad; there was always extra food to be found in the country.' I nodded, listening carefully for other sounds. Then the door began to open softly.

'How did you get out of the country?' I asked.

'When the war was over I had enough money to buy a little boat. We sailed it across the Channel and then travelled mostly on foot. We were lucky. We found an old man, an Italian; he was dying and we cared for him. When he died we took his papers. The old man's name was Antonio Scarpa. That is the name we are known by here.' Stanley always could move silently when he chose to and Alda never heard a thing. The first he knew was when Stanley's huge arm reached over and plucked the gun out of his hand. Then Stanley picked up the American and tossed him casually against the wall. Before the gunman had slid to the floor I had taken the gun from Stanley.

'Hello, Harry,' Stanley said.

'Hello, Stanley. Thank you.'

He grinned hugely. Behind him Selena came into the room.

'Are you all right?' she asked.

'Yes, what happened?'

'We saw Martinelli look out of the door and I told Stanley to get moving. We stopped just down the road and came back on foot. We were trying to decide what to do when we saw a car come out. Martinelli was driving and I thought I saw Frank Capelli.'

'You did. And his brother Tony.'

'Then he is alive?'

'Yes. This is his wife, Mary, or rather Maria now.' I turned to the older woman.

'Where have they gone?' I asked her.

'Why? So you can get a share of nothing?' she said.

'No, for Christ's sake, we can get to them before Frank kills your husband. He will, when he has the money . . .' Then her last words finally penetrated.

'What do you mean a share of nothing?' I asked.

'There is nothing. The fortune, it is gone.'

'What happened?'

'We took what we needed to buy the vineyard and this factory, and our house in the village. That wasn't very much, not then. Then we gave away all the rest.'

'You gave it away?'

'Yes.'

'Who to?'

'To charity. Not the church; they are rich enough. We gave it to charities here and on the mainland. It was the best we could think of to make some restitution for what the money had cost others.'

'So when they get to wherever he's taking them, there'll be nothing?'

'Nothing.'

'Do you know where they've gone?'

She hesitated and then seemed to reach a decision. 'I think so. Tony said it was safer than Neptune's treasure. There is a grotto at the northern end of the island, on Capo Caccia. It is called Neptune's Grotto.'

'Come on,' I shouted. 'Let's get after them. Stanley, bring our friend, and be careful. He still has a knife.' I led the way down the stairs. 'Where is the stock-room?' I asked Maria. She pointed. I unlocked the door, and the silence in the room ended in a burst of babbling talk as seven people started speaking at once.

'Tell them to call the local police and hand over our friend,' I told Maria. 'Don't tell them where we're going.' She spoke quickly to the oldest of the men and I glanced warningly at Selena. She shook her head to indicate that Maria had said nothing to affect us. Then I led the way out to the Fiat. I told Stanley to drive, and opened the rear door for Maria Capelli and Selena. I slid in beside Stanley and turned to the woman.

'Directions,' I said.

'Down into the village,' she said. 'Then turn left when we join the road. After that keep going. Drive carefully. The road is difficult.'

'Carefully, but fast,' I said.

CHAPTER TWENTY-THREE

Any reservations Maria Capelli had about my motives for getting to her husband seemed to have gone, and she snapped directions to Stanley like a navigator in an international rally. She knew the road well, and her instructions were clear, and gave him all the advance warning he needed for awkward bends and unsighted humps in the road. And there were plenty of both. The ride was terrifying when it wasn't merely hair-raising. It was almost three hours of sustained terror for me, and I think for Selena. Maria Capelli seemed impervious to it, but then she had a need to get there quickly, a need greater than ours. As for Stanley, I could not recall ever seeing him in quite the same state as he was during that drive. He was enjoying it; his smile was testimony to that. It was a different smile from the one he wore normally. It wasn't the open, pleased smile that concealed the vacancy of his mind; it seemed instead to be a smile recording true pleasure at doing something he could do as well, if not better, than anyone else. And I have to admit he did a far better job of driving that day than I could have done.

The signs advising our approach to Alghero were the first place names that meant anything to me. Then Maria's directions became more frequent as she directed Stanley through the outskirts of the city, and they also became more urgent as she sensed we were closing on the car that held her husband and his captors. I had no idea how far ahead they were.

Probably not very far; I doubted that Martinelli would have driven as fast as Stanley had done. In any event they would have had to rely on Tony Capelli's directions, and he had no incentive to get to their destination as quickly as we had. It crossed my mind that there was a distinct possibility that we had overtaken them by going on a shorter route, but I couldn't risk waiting in case we had not. When we stopped I took a few moments to steady myself; my leg muscles had been tensed since the beginning of the journey.

'Where will he have taken them?' I asked.

'Probably straight into the grotto,' she answered.

'How do we get in?'

'There are two ways. One by sea, but that's only possible in a flat calm. The other way is down the Escala del Cabriol.'

'What's that?'

'It's a staircase cut into the rock. Over there.'

'What is there when we get down?'

'The grotto is a great cave; inside there is a lake. Across the lake there are dozens of passages leading into more caves, some with lakes. The entire hillside is a honeycomb. He could take them down any of them.'

'Why would he?'

'To try to surprise them in the darkness – I don't know.' For a moment her self-control deserted her and tears glistened from her eyes. 'He may try to take the gun away from that man Martinelli.'

'Let's hope he doesn't,' I said. 'Okay. You all stay here. I'll go down and see what I can find.'

'You're not going alone?' Selena sounded concerned and I grinned at her.

'Not exactly,' I held up Alda's gun. 'I'm taking a friend.'

'But . . .' I turned away and looked at the sky, and glanced at my watch.

'It will take me nearly an hour to get down there and find my way around. Pity I haven't a torch. I might need one.'

'There will be some artificial light. For the tourists,' Maria said.

'Christ, will there be tourists down there?'

'It's getting late. They will be leaving, probably by sea. It's calm enough.'

I turned away and ran towards the steps. At the top I looked back at the three of them: the small plump woman, the slim and beautiful girl, and looming over them the huge bulk of Stanley. I waved a hand with a casualness I didn't feel and started down the steps. I had gone down about fifty or so when I heard a shout from above. I saw Selena pointing out to sea. I looked, and there was a small boat coming in towards the bottom of the cliff. There were three men in it. I stopped where I was and watched. The distance was great but Frank Capelli's black suit was easy to identify. As far as I could see none of them looked up, and even if they had done so it was unlikely they would have seen me. I waited until the boat disappeared from sight and started down again. After more than another hundred steps I stopped to catch my breath; hurrying down steps may not be as exhausting as hurrying up, but it still absorbs energy. I heard a sound above me and looked up. Stanley was following me down. I waved to him to go back but he didn't. I waited for him to reach me.

'What the hell are you doing? I told you to wait at the top.'

He smiled uncomfortably at me. 'Selena said I had to come in case you needed me,' he told me.

'Since when do you do as Selena tells you?' I demanded.

He grinned with embarrassment. 'She's nice, Harry. I think she's worried about you.'

'Christ. Okay, I can't force you to go back. Come on then, but for God's sake keep out of the way when we get down there.' I turned away and started off down the steps once again. It took less time than I had expected, but even so I was in no condition for a fight when we reached the bottom.

It would have been hopeless, but they had lit the flares the guides used to show tourists around. Presumably Frank Capelli was taking no chances in case he needed to get out unaided. As it was, when we entered the huge chamber Tony's wife had described, we could see clearly. The surface of the lake was faintly rippled and there, on the far shore, was a rowing boat. It seemed a reasonable assumption that the three men had used it to cross to the far side. Maria had guessed correctly; he was taking them towards the caves and passageways. There were four small rowing boats still at the near side of the lake. Stanley and I pushed one off, and I let him row as I sat watching the approaching shoreline. There was only one of the guide flares visible and the flickering light cast an uneasy illumination across the water. If anyone had chosen that moment to start shooting we would have been like targets on a fairground sideshow.

We reached the shore, and I left Stanley to pull the boat ashore as I tried to get some idea of where our quarry had gone. For a few moments I heard nothing and then, faintly, I heard voices. I moved in the direction of the sound, and Stanley followed me. When I was certain from which tunnel the sounds were coming I held up my hand.

'Stay here,' I whispered. 'Don't come after me, but watch out for us if we all come back together. The man we are helping, that lady's husband, is wearing a grey woollen shirt. The other two are in suits. Okay?'

'Okay, Harry.'

I moved off, and then on impulse I looked back at him. There was no smile, and he looked almost as mature as his size suggested. Almost but not quite. When he saw me looking at him the smile returned. I waved my hand and went off down the tunnel.

Ahead of me there was more noise, as if the three men were confident no one was following them. I suppose they had reason to feel that way. When I caught sight of them they were at the far side of a large chamber in the rock. Not as big as the one with the lake, but still large. Two of them were clambering up the rock-face towards an opening about four feet square. Tony Capelli was in the lead and Martinelli was close behind him. Frank Capelli made no attempt to climb the face. I heard his voice clearly.

'I will stay here, Nico,' he said. 'You see what is there and come back and tell me.'

Martinelli nodded, and the two men disappeared into the tunnel. I watched Frank Capelli carefully as he looked around for somewhere to sit. He picked a place where he could see the opening the two men had gone into. That put him with his back to me. I moved slowly towards him, watching the ground carefully to ensure I did not disturb a loose stone. I was within fifteen feet of him before he turned his head and saw me. I covered the next eight feet in two long strides and stood there, Alda's gun pointing at the thickest part of his body. I've never had to use a pistol, but I don't think even I could have missed at that range. I think he thought so too. He opened his mouth to speak but I stopped him with a gesture.

'If you speak at all, speak softly,' I said.

'Congratulations, Mr Morgan,' he said calmly. 'You said you wanted a job. You have one. Any man who can take a gun away from Alda is worthy of a place in my organisation.' I didn't tell him I had had help. 'Is Alda dead?' he asked. He didn't sound very interested.

'No,' I told him. 'By now he will be under arrest.' He looked at me and for an instant there was some emotion in his black eyes. It wasn't an emotion I liked the look of.

'So, you have handed him over to the police. Then you lied when you said you wanted to work for me. Did you also lie when you said your work for Giorgio had ended?'

'No. All he wanted to know was whether Tony was alive

or dead. Maybe, with his own death near, he was softening up. Either that or he wanted to increase his chances of going through the right gates– if he believes in that kind of thing.'

'Yes he does,' he said quietly. Maybe he did too. 'Can I buy you off?' he asked conversationally.

'No,' I said.

'So you want it all for yourself?'

'All what?'

'My father's treasure.'

'There isn't any treasure.' He looked at me flatly. 'Tony told you that to get you down here,' I said. 'I think he hopes to . . .' There was a sudden hard, echoing crack from the tunnel the two men had gone into. Capelli didn't look round.

'It sounds as if he has tried,' he said. I looked at him. There was no trace of emotion. I stayed where I was for a moment, and then I moved slowly towards the rock face, keeping the same distance between me and him. When I was close to the face and out of sight of anyone looking out of the tunnel entrance, I whispered to him.

'Stand up and face the tunnel. Say nothing. Do nothing.' He did as I ordered and we waited. I heard someone moving back along the passageway. He was making a lot of noise. Then a voice called out, the words slightly distorted by the echo from the chamber.

'It's here. I've got it.' The voice was Martinelli's. Above me I saw a movement. Martinelli came backwards out of the hole, dragging with him a heavy wooden box. He reached the level surface of the chamber floor and turned towards Capelli. I couldn't see anything in Capelli's eyes but Martinelli did. He whirled round, his gun appearing in his hand. I pulled the trigger of Alda's gun. The crash of the explosion was deafening. My shot hit Martinelli high in the chest and he was catapulted backwards. I shook my head to rid my ears of the ringing the explosion had caused. Then I moved forward, carefully watching Capelli. I reached Martinelli and looked down at him. His eyes were open and he had a peculiar, fixed expression on his face, half smile, half grimace of pain. Then his eyes closed. I watched the rise and fall of his chest. It was regular and it seemed as if I had managed to avoid killing him. I was surprised how relieved I felt about that. I took a deep breath and turned back to the opening. I knew that somehow I had to get in there and find Tony Capelli. After a moment I nodded at Frank Capelli.

'Take off your tie,' I told him. After he had done so I pointed at his feet. 'Tie your ankles together. And do it right.' Absurdly I noticed that he did have black silk socks, and his shoes did seem to be hand-made, but he didn't look quite as smart as before. When I was sure he had done as instructed I bent down and took Martinelli's tie and bound Capelli's hands tightly behind his back. I checked that he had done the job on his ankles as well as was necessary. Then I pushed Alda's gun into my waistband and scrambled into the tunnel.

I heard Tony Capelli before I found him. His breathing was heavy and laboured. When I reached him he was sitting, propped against the wall of the tunnel. Beside him in a small chamber cut in the rock were four more boxes like the one Martinelli had dragged out with him. I looked round the passage in the light from a guide flare. The passage floor looked well worn, as if it was a regular thoroughfare. I thought for a moment, then I knelt by his side.

'How bad is it?'

'I think I'll live,' he said, and tried to smile. It wasn't very successful. I pulled away his shirt and looked at the wound. He was probably right, provided I got him to a doctor fairly quickly; or a doctor to him if that seemed to be the best way. I pointed at the boxes.

'What's in them?' I asked. 'And don't tell me it's your father's treasure.' He managed another smile and this time it was an improvement on the first one.

'I saw them here,' he said. 'I recognised them as the boxes the guides use to keep their ropes and rope ladders in. There are some deep potholes farther on. Occasionally people need to be rescued. I told Martinelli it was my father's treasure. He was too greedy. He believed me and when he reached for them I tried to take his gun. I didn't succeed.' I nodded and opened the first box. As he had said, it was filled with ropes. 'Don't you believe me?' he asked.

'Yes, I'm looking for anything that will help you. Medical supplies, bandages.' I opened the next box and there was an oilskin-wrapped package laid on the top of the ropes. I opened it and took out a bandage and a packet of dry lint. It took me several minutes to take off his shirt and bandage his shoulder as well as I could.

'Do you think you can reach the chamber back there?' I asked him.

'I can try,' he said. With me leading, and helping him where he needed the leverage his wounded shoulder would not give him, we made slow progress towards the tunnel entrance. It took a long time. When we got there I peered out into the chamber. Frank Capelli was exactly where I had left him. I helped Tony down to the floor and made him comfortable against the rock face.

'Can you go farther, or do you want to stay here while I go for help?' I asked him. Another, familiar voice cut into the air.

'No need for that, Harry. Help has already arrived.' I turned round slowly and looked at Ed Kusborski. The gun in his hand was as steady as the rock he leaned against. I moved slightly and his face hardened. 'Careful, Harry. Drop whatever you used to shoot Martinelli.' I took the gun from my waistband and dropped it carefully on the ground. Kusborski grinned. 'There now. That's much better. Now we can talk,' he said.

CHAPTER TWENTY-FOUR

'I see you got my message,' I said.

Kusborski raised one eyebrow. 'Message?'

'I asked Peters to tell the NYPD we knew the records used to identify the skeleton were phoney.'

'Did you? So that's what started things moving.'

I looked at him curiously. 'Are you telling me you didn't know.'

'About the skeleton? No, I didn't know it wasn't Tony's. I assumed it wasn't, but I didn't have any proof.'

'But . . .'

'What skeleton?' Tony Capelli interrupted. I turned towards him. He didn't look as if the cold air in the cave was improving his health.

'One we found in a wood near Cobham in Surrey.'

He nodded his head slowly. 'So that's what started it all up again. After all these years I thought Gerry was hidden for ever. Do you know who it was?'

'Yes, your friend Gerry Brown.'

'That's right.'

'Did you kill him?'

'No.' His voice hardened suddenly and he pointed his good arm at his brother. 'My brother killed him.' Frank Capelli turned his blank look on his brother and then turned away again. 'They came to England,' Tony went on. 'My brother Franco and one of his men, Mike D'Angelo. He wanted the number on my medallion. They came to me that night. I was with Gerry Brown. They took both of us into the woods there and they tried to make me tell them the number. I wouldn't so they threatened to kill Gerry.' His voice became softer. 'I thought it was a bluff. It wasn't. He cut Gerry's throat. Him. My beloved brother. I thought it had to be a bluff. No member of the family had ever killed before. I broke away and ran deeper into the woods. D'Angelo followed and I backtracked and came up on him from behind. We struggled. His gun went off but neither of us was hurt. Then I knocked him out and went after my brother. He had heard the shot and I could hear him calling for D'Angelo. When there was no reply he knew I had the gun, so he ran. I chased him but he got away. Then I went back to D'Angelo. I didn't know what to do but I knew I needed time until I could make plans. I made D'Angelo put on Gerry's uniform and we buried the body. I put D'Angelo's clothes and his wallet and his ring in the grave. Then I made him come back to the camp with me. My idea was to get him into the camp that night so that the roll-call would show Gerry was still alive, and then get him out again the next morning. Then, when Gerry was found to be missing, it would not be tied to me. We got into the camp okay. Gerry was much taller than D'Angelo but no one noticed. The place was in uproar. We'd been mobilised. I panicked. I gave D'Angelo one of my uniforms – it fitted him better than Gerry's – and I told him I would get him away the first chance I could. Then, before I could do anything, we were on the aircraft and taking off. You know what happened. It crashed and I was thrown clear. I knew a few others were alive too. I could see them and D'Angelo wasn't among them. So when the plane blew up I ran for it. I went to Mary and . . .'

'I know about that,' I said. 'So your brother Frank was the only man who knew the skeleton was Gerry Brown's?'

'Yes.' I looked at Frank Capelli.

'So why did you try to make it appear to be Tony's?' I asked him. He looked at me with the same flat stare he had used on his brother, and then turned away again. Kusborski straightened up and moved away from the wall he had been leaning against.

'Because he guessed that it was the man he had killed and he wanted to be certain people wouldn't dig too deep,' he said.

'But why Tony?'

'He was covering all angles. If Tony was still alive he wanted to find him, and if people thought the body was Tony's they would stop looking. That way he had a clear field.'

'Why are you here?' I asked.

'Two reasons. We'll deal with one of them now.' He looked at Tony Capelli.

'Where is Joe Capelli's fortune? Or is it all spent?'

'It is all gone,' Tony answered wearily. 'Not spent, just gone.'

'Where?'

'I don't suppose you will believe me any more than the others, but I gave it away – to charity.'

Kusborski looked at him carefully for a moment and then he began to laugh.

'You know something? I think I do believe you.' He looked at Frank Capelli. 'How do you like that Franco? All that trouble, and all for nothing.' Capelli looked at him bleakly. Then he spat on the floor of the cave. Kusborski grinned cheerfully. 'Okay, so let's tidy things up,' he said. He pointed his gun at me. 'Harry, you take off. Stanley is back there. I had to tap him on the head but he should be coming round now. Take him and get out of here.'

'Why?'

'Why? Because I've no quarrel with you.'

'You'll need help getting these men to the surface,' I said. 'Two of them are injured, seriously. We'll need doctors and the police.'

'No doctors, Harry, and no police. Remember me? I'm your friendly neighbourhood cop.' I looked at him carefully and I looked even more carefully at the gun in his hand. I shook my head slowly.

'No, Ed. If you're going to kill me, do it now, while I'm looking at you, not when I'm walking away from you. If I'm about to get shot I don't want it in the back.' He looked at me, and there was an odd expression in his eyes. Suddenly I saw a slight movement and I forced myself not to move my eyes to see it more clearly. Then the movement came again and I knew it was Martinelli. He was slowly and gently sliding his fingers inside his jacket. Kusborski was unsighted and I thought desperately of some way to keep him looking my way without making him start shooting. 'You can't kill us all,' I said, thinking dully that he intended doing just that.

'I think I shall have to, Harry,' he said and there was a slight hint of regret in his voice.

'Christ, there are four of us,' I said.

'More than that,' he said. 'I'll have to deal with Stanley too, and Selena Cantrell. I expect she's here. Oh and then there's Mario Alda. What have you done with him, by the way?' I saw a small ray of hope.

'The police have him and they will be following us here,' I said. 'You would never get away with it, Ed. When they arrive here and there's only you and a pile of corpses, how will you talk your way out of that?'

'I'm a police officer and these are all criminals,' he waved his hand in a dismissive gesture.

'I'm not. Stanley's not. He's not,' I said, pointing at Tony Capelli.

'I'll see to it that the guns I use on you and Stanley belong to Alda and Martinelli, that will settle the minds of the local police.'

Behind me I saw Martinelli's hand come out of his jacket; there was a knife in it. Short-bladed, it looked like a throwing knife, and I hoped it was because there was no other way it could be used. Martinelli drew back his arm and as he did so a grunt of pain was forced from his lips. Kusborski spun round, but he mistook the source of the noise and he fired at Frank Capelli. The roar of the gun echoed in the enclosed space and I started forward, crouched low, and at the same instant Martinelli threw the knife. Kusborski was already turning to meet me when the knife caught him, slicing through the sleeve of his jacket and embedding itself in his forearm. His gun fell from his hand and he tried to grab for it with his other hand. That was when I reached him, and the two of us struggled together on the hard, cold floor of the cave. I kicked the gun away and hit him hard in the stomach. He doubled over and I made a dive for the gun he had made me drop. I didn't reach it. He recovered and flung himself at my legs. I went down and my head hit the floor. For a moment there was blackness mingled with the flickering light of the flare that illuminated the cave. Then my head cleared and I started to get to my feet, but he had already reached the gun. He straightened up, and there was a gleam in his eyes, as the gun came level with my chest, which told me that this time nothing was going to stop him pulling the trigger. At that instant a huge black shape hurled itself from the darkness and seemed to envelop Kusborski. He did pull the trigger but the bullet whistled harmlessly past my ear. I ran forward, aware as I did so of the sound of the gun clattering to the floor as Stanley straightened up. For an instant I couldn't see Kusborski. Then I realised that Stanley was holding him, his long, strong arms wrapped around his middle. Kusborski was a big man and a strong one, but he looked like a small child as he struggled ineffectually to free himself from Stanley's grasp, his arms and legs flailing uselessly at the air. I reached them and took hold of Stanley's arm.

'Okay, Stanley, drop him now.' Nothing happened and in the flickering light I saw Kusborski's face discolouring. I pulled at Stanley's arms, shouting at him to drop Kusborski, but he didn't, and then as I pulled and shouted and beat at his arms I heard a hideous cracking sound and with it a choking, liquid gurgle. The sound was coming from Kusborski's mouth. Then the noise stopped, and after a moment the cracking sound stopped too.

It took me several more minutes before I made Stanley release Kusborski. When, finally, he did release him, the big American dropped loosely to the ground. He didn't move and he didn't make a sound. I knew that he was dead before I knelt beside him to try and find a pulse. I made Stanley sit down well away from the body, and I went back to the others. Tony Capelli didn't look any worse and I reckoned he would live. Martinelli was unconscious. The effort of throwing the knife at Kusborski had been too much for him. The wound where my bullet had hit him seemed to have stopped bleeding. I thought he would live too. Frank Capelli was in worse shape. Kusborski's bullet had hit him in the chest and there was a massive exit hole in his back. It was a miracle he was alive at all, and I put his chances of surviving as too low to be worth thinking about. He was still bound hand and foot, as I had left him, and I untied the two neckties I had used and tried to make him comfortable. I don't think it made any difference; he was in shock, and looked like staying that way to the end. Then, surprisingly his eyes opened and they looked at me with the same flat black stare.

'I thought Kusborski was working for you,' I said, aware of the foolishness of talking to him at that time. For the first time the eyes took on a readable expression. Hatred.

'Gizzo,' he said, and the hatred was matched in the voice.

Then the black eyes lost their expression, and after a moment they went dull and slowly closed. He was dead. I stood up and walked around gathering up the armoury. I went back to Tony Capelli and helped him into a more comfortable position.

'I'll go for help,' I told him. 'I don't think Martinelli will give you any trouble. If he does, tell him there's a way out for him if he co-operates.'

'What way out?'

I shook my head. 'I haven't worked it out yet, but I'll think of one.'

'Why do you want a way out for him?'

'Because if I don't find a way out for him, and for Alda, then the whole world will know that you're Tony Capelli, and worse,' I waved my hand towards where Stanley was still sitting, 'the whole world will know that Stanley killed a man.' I looked at him hard. 'I don't give a damn who knows about you but I do care about him.' He read the expression in my eyes and nodded his head without speaking. I left Martinelli's gun with him and walked over to Stanley.

'Come on,' I said. 'You can't sit around here all day.' He looked up at me unsmilingly, and then the smile slowly returned.

'Can we go out of here, Harry? It isn't very nice is it?'

'No, Stanley,' I said. 'It isn't very nice.' I walked back across the floor of the cave and into the tunnel that led to the main chamber of the underground lake. Stanley followed me. I let him row the boat, and I let him help me up the last of the steps carved in the cliffside. Someone told me afterwards that there were over six hundred and fifty of them. It seemed like ten times that number.

CHAPTER TWENTY-FIVE

The story I thought up was full of holes but it held up – just. We told the police that Alda, Martinelli and Frank Capelli were trying to rob Tony. Alda and Martinelli told the same story. They had a lot more to lose than a short stay in a Sardinian prison for attempted robbery. We told the police that Selena and Stanley and me were on holiday, and had just stumbled into the robbery and were carried along with it. Tony Capelli said he had tricked the three men into believing that he had money hidden in the caves on the Capo Caccia in order to get them away from his wife. After that we told the story more or less the way it was, except that we said Kusborski was an accomplice, and had joined them at the caves, and they had fallen out and fought amongst themselves. I don't think the Sardinian police really believed very much of it but we all said the same thing, and they couldn't work out why three seemingly unconnected groups of people would collaborate to fake a story. Especially when one of the groups, Alda and Martinelli, would end up in prison.

I called Peters the first chance I got and elicited a half promise from him to play things down, and that he would try and get New York to do the same. I told him enough over the telephone for him to convince them that to do otherwise would cast yet another slur on New York's Finest. He said he would want to see me when I got back. It wasn't a request.

There was one other lie I told the police. That was one I am sure they didn't believe, but again they couldn't figure out why anyone would admit to a killing he hadn't really done. They kept looking at me and my normal arms and then at Stanley and his massive arms, and then they looked at the doctor's report on how Kusborski had died. They shook their heads a lot but eventually they let us go. They made it clear that the sooner we left the island the sooner they would be able to smile again. They also made it plain we would not be expected back.

Maria Capelli turned out to be a superb cook. I think I would have been disappointed if she hadn't been. It was the first time she had cooked a real English meal for years, and she revelled in it, and so did Stanley. After we had eaten, Capelli found a bottle of brandy that looked as if it deserved a more discerning palate than mine, but I didn't tell him so. It didn't look as if I would get very much out of the case and I felt that at least I deserved a decent drink.

'Where was the old man's fortune hidden?' I asked.

'In a house in the village,' Tony said. 'We came to Laconi by a process of elimination. Much as you did, although it took us longer because we didn't have Giorgio's number. There was a house just opposite the church. It was called the Villa Santini. My father's buffer must have had a sense of humour. The money was buried in the cellar. We bought the house and we live there now. We changed the name though.'

'You took a chance calling your wine Rosa Medaglione.'

'That was an impulse. Foolish perhaps but it didn't seem to matter.'

'Why did Kusborski do what he did?' Selena asked.

'I'm not certain,' I said. 'I asked Frank before he died and he said one word. Gizzo.'

'Fiore Gizzo?' Capelli asked. 'Is he still alive?'

'Yes,' Selena answered. 'And there is no sign that he

intends letting go of the organisation.' She turned to me. 'Do you think Kusborski was Gizzo's man?'

'I think he must have been. Frank had access to NYPD information. I thought it was through Kusborski but it seems it wasn't. He certainly wasn't working for himself so that only leaves Gizzo. I don't know why.'

'He was the only one who would benefit from seeing the Capelli brothers out the way,' Selena said. 'He didn't know about Giorgio.' She looked at Tony Capelli. 'I can't promise not to tell your brother you're still alive,' she said.

He nodded. 'I cannot prevent you, but . . .' He shrugged and the shrug seemed to say he hoped she would not. I decided to talk to her later. I could see no reason to risk Tony's and his wife's privacy, or even their lives, if Gizzo should find they were still alive.

'Pity about Kusborski,' I said. 'I liked him, even though all the time I thought he was working for Frank.'

'All the time?' Selena asked.

'Most of the time,' I amended. 'I suspected something from that time you and Mason came to the cottage. Mason called him Sergeant, which meant that they knew each other although neither of them admitted it. Then when I saw Mason with Alda and Martinelli, the only person around who could have hit me was Kusborski. The next day he had a cut hand, and somebody had broken a window to start the burglar alarm. He must have done that to create a diversion while he got Mason's body away.'

'You mean he killed John?'

'He must have done, Alda and Martinelli both used .32 Smith & Wessons. Kusborski used a .44. Mason was killed with a .44. If Peters gets a ballistics report from the Sardinian police he can check. I talked to Martinelli in the hospital. He said Mason had gone to them to try to set up a deal with Frank. Mason said he would get the number of Giorgio's medallion from you.' I grinned at her. 'He overrated himself. They said they would consider the deal and pass it on to Frank. Mason was out of the room while I was at the lower-floor window. He must have been upstairs and Kusborski would have seen him when he looked through the upstairs window. He must have realised that whatever deal he had going with Mason, Mason was trying a double-cross. So he killed him.' I finished my drink and stood up. 'What time is the flight tomorrow?' I asked.

'Eight o'clock,' Selena said.

'We'd better get an early night then,' I told her. She stood up and we said our good-byes to the Capellis. I shook Tony Capelli by the hand, as I did so a thought struck me.

'Did you keep your medallion?' I asked. 'Or did you throw it away after you had found the hiding place?'

'I lost it,' he said. 'In the wood when I was chasing Mike D'Angelo.'

'So it is there, somewhere?'

'Yes.'

'Maybe it will turn up one day then.'

'I doubt it,' he said. 'Not after all these years.' I looked at him.

'Some things have turned up,' I said. 'It seems that the saying is right – you can't bury the past.'

'There's a saying here,' he said: 'God is already too busy. Sometimes he needs help from man, especially when injustice has to be punished.'

'Is that what you think happened?' I said. I looked at his wife. 'Any messages for anyone?' I asked. She looked at her husband and then at me. She shook her head.

'You mean Mrs Kenny. Perhaps it would be wisest to say nothing,' she said.

'I expect you're right,' I said. I don't know whether I believed what I said, and I don't know if she did either.

The three of us went back to the car and I drove to the

motel at Pirri. Selena was silent most of the way, but as we turned into the motel she touched my shoulder.

'You know my connection at Rome is only a few minutes after we land.'

'Yes,' I said.

'So when we say good-bye tonight it will be for the last time.'

'Yes,' I said again. After I had parked the car I went across to our room with Stanley. When he was in bed I turned out the light and went to the door.

'Harry.' I stopped.

'Yes, Stanley?'

'Selena is a nice lady isn't she?'

'Yes, Stanley, she is.'

'Why don't you marry her?' he asked. I was silent for a moment.

'I don't know, Stanley. Do you think I should?'

'Yes, that would be nice.' I closed the door and walked across to Selena's room.

Making love to someone for the first time is often a total mess. Neither one knows the other's likes and dislikes, sensitive places and insensitive places. Occasionally, very occasionally, it can be perfect. That night it was perfect. Afterwards I remembered Stanley's question.

'Stanley thinks we should get married.'

She moved lazily in the bed. 'What does Harry think?' she asked.

'Harry thinks it would be a good idea too. What does Selena think?'

'I think . . .' The telephone by the bedside rang fiercely. She reached out and picked it up. 'Yes.' There was silence as she listened to the speaker at the other end. Then she said good-bye and hung up.

'Who was it?' I asked. She didn't answer. 'Was it Giorgio?'

'Giorgio is dead,' she said. I didn't say anything for a moment.

'Then you don't have to go back to New York,' I said after a moment. She said nothing, and then I heard a faint muffled sound from the pillow beside me. She was crying. It was some time before she had recovered sufficiently to speak.

'He tried to be a good man, towards the end,' she said. I didn't answer; after all, what is good to one person might be something very different to another. 'At first he thought the discovery of the skeleton might lead him to his father's hoard of gold and silver. Then he changed. He wanted to know if his youngest brother was alive or dead. That day he spoke to you on the telephone, he meant what he said.'

I waited, and when she didn't speak again I thought it might be a good moment to ask the question I had asked earlier.

'There is nothing to take you back now. You could come to England instead of going back to New York. You don't have to go back now, do you?'

'Yes, Harry, I have to. There is the funeral and there'll be other things and . . .'

'And after that?'

'After that, I don't know, Harry.' There are some questions you should never ask. Among them are those which you know will have answers you don't want to hear.

CHAPTER TWENTY-SIX

Very little had changed when I got back to the office. On the desk there was more dust than there had been before. And there was a little pile of bills that I glanced at before filing in the 'forget' drawer. Then I rang Peters and told him I was back. He suggested I should go and see him, and I did. I told him slightly more of the truth than I had told the Sardinian police. In fact I told him everything except who had really killed Kusborski. Fowler was there, sneering. When I got to the part about the big American the sneer faded a little. Maybe he thought I might like to practise on an English variety of police sergeant. Between them they made a lot of notes, and then they told me to go back the next day and sign various statements they would be having typed. I said I would. I didn't like loose ends any more than they did.

When I got back to the office the telephone was ringing. It was Mike Silver.

'The woman in Devon, the one we were chasing for money.'

'What about her?' I asked.

'The job you did for her, did it have anything to do with her daughter?'

'Why?'

'Did you see yesterday's paper?'

'No, I've been away. What's happened?'

'The daughter is dead. She took an overdose of sleeping

pills.' I remembered the girl as I had last seen her. Sitting in a railway compartment, looking sad and lost but with just a tiny gleam of hope in her eyes. Hope I had put there. I tried to convince myself that if I had left her alone she would still have killed herself, but in a Battersea basement instead of in glorious Devon. I wasn't very successful. 'Are you still there?' Mike's voice came from far away. I listened to him breathing at the other end of the telephone.

'No,' I said eventually. 'It didn't have anything to do with the daughter.'

'Thank God for that,' he said. After he had hung up I looked at the wall and decided I liked the office the way it had been. I rearranged the furniture and went up the High Street to buy a picture to cover the damp patch. I bought one of an elephant that looked as if it was about to charge the painter – or get shot. The shop was just across the way from the White Horse, and I went in for a drink. The clientele still seemed to be a few hundred years younger than me. One of them was Rosemary. She was with a tall young man in high-heeled boots and a denim suit. She seemed to be trying to climb up his legs. She looked at me once, briefly, as I stood up to leave. There was no sign in her eyes that she had ever seen me before.

When I got back to the office I hung the picture on the wall and then sat at my desk and looked at it. I decided that the elephant was about to charge. Nobody could have wanted to shoot it. I was still sitting there when the telephone rang. It was Selena.

'How are you, Harry?'

'Well enough,' I said.

'Giorgio's affairs are being settled. He left instructions for a payment to be made if you settled the matter of his brother Tony.' From her voice I knew that someone else was in the room with her.

'So?'

'I have told his attornies that you were satisfied that Tony Capelli died in the plane crash.'

'Oh,' I said.

'If you will send in your report to that effect they can release what Giorgio left.'

'Oh,' I said again.

'It's ten thousand dollars, Harry.'

'Are you coming back here?' I asked.

'You will send the report then?'

'Are you coming back?'

'No. That will not be possible.'

'Never?'

'Never.'

'I see. There's nothing else to say then.'

'You will send your report?' Selena repeated. I looked at the telephone in my hand, and then carefully replaced it on its rest. After a few minutes I picked it up again and dialled Julie's number. A man answered.

'Is that Paul Jackson?' I asked.

'No it isn't. This is Mrs Matthews's house and my name's Martin Govan. Who is speaking?' He didn't sound very pleased and I thought fast. I had no right to spoil any more of Julie's attempts to find happiness.

'That isn't the Bramley Golf Club?' I said.

'No it isn't,' he said, sounding a shade happier.

'Very sorry to have bothered you,' I said and hung up. I looked at the elephant. It wasn't about to charge anyone. It was about to get shot.

I was late getting home that night and I had made several calls on the way. I wasn't drunk. But the alcohol level in my blood was high enough to have made me a fire hazard. Stanley was waiting at the door.

'You're late, Harry,' he said. I nodded. Speech seemed too great an effort. I followed him into the kitchen.

'I'll get your dinner,' I said and then he stood aside. I

looked at the kitchen table. It was laid for two. Not well laid; the cutlery was all wrong, and no plates matched, but it was still laid. There were some sandwiches that appeared to have been chopped out of the loaf with an axe. There was something cooking on the stove. It smelled as if cooking was the last thing it wanted. Stanley was beaming at me.

'What's going on?' I asked.

'I've made the dinner for us, Harry.'

'Why? I mean, thank you, Stanley. But why?'

'Because it's your birthday,' he said. I thought about it. He was right, it was. He took something from the top of a cupboard. It was a package, fairly neatly wrapped and tied up with a ribbon. He handed it to me and I took it, standing there, feeling slightly foolish.

'What is it?'

'Your birthday present, Harry.' I sat down at the table and after a moment I unwrapped the package. It was a small metal cigarette box, the kind they used years ago. I looked at it. 'I found it on the site Harry.'

'Thank you, Stanley. It's very nice.'

'Not the box, Harry. That's just a box out of my collection. Your present's inside.' I opened the box. After about forty years I found the strength to speak.

'Where did you get it, Stanley?'

'I told you, Harry, I found it on the site.'

'When?'

'Oh ages ago, when we first went there. I was in the woods one day looking at birds, and I found it. I knew you would like it, so I hid it away where no one could find it, so I could give it to you today. You do like it, don't you, Harry?' I tilted the box so that my birthday present dropped out into my hand. I don't know whether or not things would have been different if he had given it to me earlier, or even if it had been found during all the searches that had been made amongst his collection. Maybe they would, maybe they wouldn't. Maybe John Mason and Frank Capelli and Ed Kusborski would have stayed alive. Maybe they would and maybe they wouldn't. I held up Tony Capelli's Rose Medallion and looked at it.

'Yes, Stanley, I do like it. I like it very much indeed. Thank you.'

His smile threatened to split his face in two, and then we both smelled burning and he jumped to the stove with a shout. It was too late. Whatever it was he had been cooking was burned. I looked at my watch.

'Never mind, Stanley,' I said. 'The fish shop will still be open. I'll treat you.' We went out and climbed into the Volvo. Then I began to feel the effect of the drinking I'd done. I made him get out while I crawled over into the passenger seat. He walked around and climbed into the driving seat and pushed it as far back as it would go. He started the engine and we went down to the road.

'Drive carefully, Stanley,' I said, just before I fell asleep.

Prices and postage and packing rates shown below were correct at the time of going to press.

FICTION

All prices shown are exclusive of postage and packing

GENERAL FICTION

☐ THE CAIN CONSPIRACY	J. M. Simmel	£1.20
☐ THE AFFAIR OF NINA B	J. M. Simmel	£1.20
☐ HMS BOUNTY	John Maxwell	£1.00
☐ A REAL KILLING	William Keegan	80p
☐ SEARCHING FOR CALEB	Anne Tyler	95p
☐ CELESTIAL NAVIGATION	Anne Tyler	95p
☐ THE ENTREPRENEUR	I. G. Broat	£1.00
☐ THE SOUNDS OF SILENCE	Judith Richards	£1.00
☐ THE BOTTOM LINE	Fletcher Knebel	£1.25
☐ ON THE BRINK	Benjamin Stein with Herbert Stein	95p
☐ CHAINS	Justin Adams	£1.20
☐ RUNNING SCARED	Gregory Mcdonald	85p
☐ V. J. DAY	Alan Fields	95p
☐ THE HEIR	Christopher Keane	£1.00
☐ THE LAREDO ASSIGNMENT (Western)	Matt Chisholm	75p
☐ TY-SHAN BAY	Raoul Templeton Aundrews	95p
☐ A SEA-CHANGE	Lois Gould	80p
☐ THE PLAYERS	Gary Brandner	95p
☐ RIDDLE	Dan Sherman	90p

CRIME/THRILLER

☐ THE TWO FACES OF JANUARY	Patricia Highsmith	95p
☐ THOSE WHO WALK AWAY	Patricia Highsmith	95p
☐ A GAME FOR THE LIVING	Patricia Highsmith	95p
☐ THE BLUNDERER	Patricia Highsmith	95p
☐ THE TREMOR OF FORGERY	Patricia Highsmith	80p
☐ STRAIGHT	Steve Knickmeyer	80p
☐ FIVE PIECES OF JADE	John Ball	85p
☐ IN THE HEAT OF THE NIGHT	John Ball	85p
☐ THE EYES OF BUDDHA	John Ball	85p
☐ THE COOL COTTONTAIL	John Ball	80p
☐ JOHNNY GET YOUR GUN	John Ball	85p
☐ THE PEKING PAY-OFF	Ian Stewart	90p
☐ THE TEN-TOLA BARS	Burton Wohl	90p
☐ FLETCH	Gregory Mcdonald	90p
☐ CONFESS, FLETCH	Gregory Mcdonald	90p
☐ THE TRIPOLI DOCUMENTS	Henry Kane	95p
☐ DEADLY HARVEST	Peter Mallory	85p
☐ THE EXECUTION	Oliver Crawford	90p
☐ FROGS AT THE BOTTOM OF THE WELL	Ken Edgar	90p
☐ TIME BOMB	James D. Atwater	90p

ROMANCE

☐ NIGHTINGALE PARK	Moira Lord	90p
☐ ROYAL FLUSH	Margaret Irwin	£1.20
☐ THE BRIDE	Margaret Irwin	£1.20
☐ THE PROUD SERVANT	Margaret Irwin	£1.25
☐ DAUGHTER OF DESTINY	Stephanie Blake	£1.25
☐ FLOWERS OF FIRE	Stephanie Blake	£1.00
☐ BLAZE OF PASSION	Stephanie Blake	£1.20
☐ LOVE'S SCARLET BANNER	Fiona Harrowe	£1.20
☐ MYSTIC ROSE	Patricia Gallagher	£1.20
☐ CAPTIVE BRIDE	Johanna Lindsey	£1.00
☐ A PIRATE'S LOVE	Johanna Lindsey	£1.20
☐ ROSELYNDE	Roberta Gellis	£1.20
☐ ALINOR	Roberta Gellis	£1.20

SCIENCE FICTION

☐ THE OTHER LOG OF PHILEAS FOGG	Philip José Farmer	80p
☐ GRIMM'S WORLD	Vernor Vinge	75p
☐ A TOUCH OF STRANGE	Theodore Sturgeon	85p
☐ THE SILENT INVADERS	Robert Silverberg	80p
☐ THE SEED OF EARTH	Robert Silverberg	80p
☐ CRITICAL THRESHOLD	Brian Stableford	75p
☐ THE FLORIANS	Brian M. Stableford	80p
☐ FURY	Henry Kuttner	80p
☐ HEALER	F. Paul Wilson	80p
☐ CAGE A MAN	F. M. Busby	75p
☐ JOURNEY	Marta Randall	£1.00

HORROR/OCCULT

☐ POE MUST DIE	Marc Olden	£1.00
☐ ISOBEL	Jane Parkhurst	£1.00
☐ THE HOWLING	Gary Brandner	85p
☐ RETURN OF THE HOWLING	Gary Brandner	85p
☐ SPIDERS	Richard Lewis	80p
☐ RETURN OF THE LIVING DEAD	John Russo	80p
☐ DYING LIGHT	Evan Chandler	85p

FILM/TV TIE IN

☐ WUTHERING HEIGHTS	Emily Brontë	80p
☐ AMERICAN GIGOLO	Timothy Harris	80p

NON-FICTION

☐ KILLING TIME	Sandy Fawkes	90p
☐ THE HAMLYN BOOK OF CROSSWORDS 1		60p
☐ THE HAMLYN BOOK OF CROSSWORDS 2		60p
☐ THE HAMLYN FAMILY GAMES BOOK	Gyles Brandreth	75p
☐ STAR-FILE ANNUAL (Ref)	Dafydd Rees	£1.50
☐ THE OSCAR MOVIES FROM A-Z (Ref)	Roy Pickard	£1.25
☐ THE HAMLYN FAMILY MEDICAL DICTIONARY (Ref)		£2.50
☐ LONELY WARRIOR (War)	Victor Houart	85p
☐ BLACK ANGELS (War)	Rupert Butler	£1.00
☐ THE BEST OF DIAL-A-RECIPE	Audrey Ellis	80p
☐ THE SUNDAY TELEGRAPH PATIO GARDENING BOOK	Robert Pearson	80p
☐ THE COMPLETE TRAVELLER	Joan Bakewell	£1.50
☐ RESTORING OLD JUNK	Michèle Brown	75p
☐ WINE MAKING AT HOME	Francis Pinnegar	80p
☐ FAT IS A FEMINIST ISSUE	Susie Orbach	85p
☐ AMAZING MAZES 1	Michael Lye	75p
☐ GUIDE TO THE CHANNEL ISLANDS	Janice Anderson and Edmund Swinglehurst	90p
☐ THE STRESS FACTOR	Donald Norfolk	90p
☐ WOMAN × TWO	Mary Kenny	90p
☐ THE HAMLYN BOOK OF CROSSWORDS 3		60p

KITCHEN LIBRARY

☐ MIXER AND BLENDER COOKBOOK	Myra Street	80p
☐ HOME BAKED BREADS AND CAKES	Mary Norwak	75p
☐ MARGUERITE PATTEN'S FAMILY COOKBOOK		95p
☐ EASY ICING	Marguerite Patten	85p
☐ HOME MADE COUNTRY WINES		40p
☐ COMPREHENSIVE GUIDE TO DEEP FREEZING		40p
☐ COUNTRY FARE	Doreen Fulleylove	80p

All these books are available at your local bookshop or newsagent, or can be ordered direct from the publisher. Just tick the titles you want and fill in the form below.

NAME..

ADDRESS..

....

Write to Hamlyn Paperbacks Cash Sales, PO Box 11, Falmouth, Cornwall TR10 9EN

Please enclose remittance to the value of the cover price plus:

UK: 22p for the first book plus 10p per copy for each additional book ordered to a maximum charge of 92p.

BFPO and EIRE: 22p for the first book plus 10p per copy for the next 6 books, thereafter 4p per book.

OVERSEAS: 30p for the first book and 10p for each additional book.

Whilst every effort is made to keep prices low it is sometimes necessary to increase cover prices and also postage and packing rates at short notice. Hamlyn Paperbacks reserve the right to show new retail prices on covers which may differ from those previously advertised in the text or elsewhere.